"Now I want it even more."

Sage slammed her eyes shut and swallowed hard, silently willing the parts of her body shifting into overdrive back into neutral. She should have stayed behind her desk with her legs tightly crossed, because this man was on the verge of talking the panties right off her.

When she opened her eyes, his gaze was locked on her lips.

"Is this your idea of keeping friends close and enemies closer?" The mocking tone she'd hoped for fell flat, and her question echoed in her ears like a breathless pant.

"You're not my enemy, Sage," Cole murmured. "You're a challenge." He brushed his knuckles down her cheek. "And I do love a challenge."

If she'd been clearheaded, a snappy comeback would have been on the tip of her tongue. However, her brain had taken the backseat in her headspace, allowing a wave of longing to take the wheel.

"That lipstick is beautiful on you." His eyes never leaving her lips, Cole swiped the pad of his thumb across a sticky spot near the corner of her mouth. Sage stood mesmerized as he slowly licked the sugary glaze from his thumb, while her imagination conjured up illicit images of him licking her everywhere.

"What's it called?" he asked.

"'Taste Me.'"

"You just read my mind." Cupping her chin in his hand, Cole leaned in and brushed his lips against hers.

Dear Reader,

At some point, we've all thought, "Life would be a lot easier if everyone was just like me."

That's exactly what Espresso Cosmetics CEO Cole Sinclair finds in rival cosmetics company owner Sage Matthews. Only nothing comes easy as Sage proves to be every bit as cocky, stubborn and competitive as he is.

I enjoyed the interaction between Cole and Sage as their sexy game of one-upmanship progresses to grudging respect, friendship and, finally, love. I hope you have as much fun reading it as I did writing it!

All my best,

Phyllis

Moonlight *Kisses*

PHYLLIS BOURNE

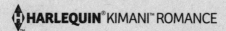

HARLEQUIN® KIMANI™ ROMANCE

Recycling programs
for this product may
not exist in your area.

ISBN-13: 978-0-373-86404-1

Moonlight Kisses

Copyright © 2015 by Phyllis Bourne Williams

Printed in U.S.A.

Phyllis Bourne is a native of Chicago's South Side and began her writing career as a newspaper crime reporter. After years of cops and criminals, she left reporting to write about life's sweeter side. Nowadays, her stories are filled with heart-stopping heroes and happy endings. When she's not writing, she can usually be found at a makeup counter feeding her lipstick addiction. You can find her on the web at www.phyllisbourne.com and facebook.com/phyllisbournebooks.

Books by Phyllis Bourne

Harlequin Kimani Romance

Taste for Temptation
Sweeter Temptation
Every Road to You
Falling into Forever
Moonlight Kisses

Visit the Author Profile page at
Harlequin.com for more titles.

For Byron

Chapter 1

"Who put the scowl on your face?"

Cole Sinclair looked up from the newspaper he'd been absorbed in to see his stepfather standing in his office doorway.

"No, don't tell me. Let me guess." Victor Gray raised a finger in a halting gesture. "Stiletto Cosmetics."

Folding the business section in half, Cole slung it across his desk in disgust. "How'd you guess?"

"If you're frowning, it usually has something to do with them."

Cole pushed away from his desk and began to pace in front of the wall of windows offering a panoramic view of downtown Nashville. He'd known when he'd returned to his hometown that reviving his family's troubled cosmetics company would be a monumental task.

The widely held opinion that Espresso Cosmetics was old-lady makeup was firmly entrenched. Moreover, an upstart cosmetics company had set up shop in town, grabbing both headlines and Espresso's dwindling customer base.

"The media's handing out good press to Stiletto like candy on Halloween," he muttered. "Meanwhile, we can barely get a reporter to return a phone call."

Victor hovered in the doorway. "They're just capitalizing on their fifteen minutes of fame since that singer mentioned them on television. It won't last much longer."

Cole wasn't so sure. Stiletto had been generating buzz on the web even before pop star Crave gave them a shout-out on national television. He stopped midpace to glance out the window. An electronic billboard in the distance stood out against the gray January skies. It flashed continuous images of a cheeseburger with toppings stacked nearly as high as Espresso's aging eleven-story building.

He stared blankly at it, his mind on how Stiletto was gaining ground with a generation of young women Espresso was desperate to attract. Unfortunately, an article in today's paper had pushed that demographic even further out of their reach.

"I stopped by to see if you wanted to go to lunch with me later," his stepfather said. "I saw a billboard of the most mouthwatering burger I've ever seen on the drive in this morning, and I've been drooling ever since."

That burger did look good, Cole thought. Real food. A lot better than the upscale dining experiences he'd endured while handling Espresso business these past months.

He also recognized that Victor's invitation was for more than lunch. His late mother's second husband, the only father he'd ever known, was extending another olive branch to help rebuild their once-close relationship after eight years of estrangement.

"Another time, Vic. I doubt I'll have an appetite by lunchtime. Dinner, either."

"So are you going to tell me what's going on or keep frowning until your face gets stuck like that?" the older man said, still hovering in the doorway.

"There's something you need to read."

Cole watched his stepfather hesitate before venturing beyond the doorway into the overhauled office that no longer bore the feminine traces of the company's founder.

Cole snatched the copy of *America Today* off the mahogany executive desk he'd brought in to replace the elegant Queen Anne writing table his mother and Espresso founder, Selina Sinclair Gray, had ruled from. Snapping it open, he pointed out the article responsible for his current mood and handed it to Victor.

He watched his stepfather's eyes narrow as he zeroed in on one of the photos accompanying the story. The older man drew the newspaper in until it nearly touched his nose.

"Wow!"

"Exactly," Cole said, still steaming over it. Then he caught an uncharacteristic gleam in Victor's eyes. It lit up his entire face. In fact, he was practically ogling the newspaper.

What the...?

"God knows I worshipped the ground your mother walked on," his stepfather said, "but would you take a look at those long legs in that short skirt and those high heels. I don't see a thing here to put a frown on a man's face."

Cole snatched the paper back from him.

Victor shook his head and a sly grin spread over his lips. "She's got a young Angela Davis thing going on with that wild Afro, too. Yes, sir! If I were five or ten years younger, she'd be your new mama."

Cole stared at the smaller photo he'd ignored before, the larger one having grabbed his attention and earned his ire.

"More like twenty-five to thirty years younger," he grumbled. "She could be your daughter."

Cole frowned at the photo of the woman sitting on the edge of a desk. So this was Stiletto's owner. His gaze drifted to the untamed mane of kinky coils surrounding a no-nonsense face and full, unsmiling lips. Sage Matthews looked exactly like what she and her company were—a pain in his ass.

He shoved the newspaper back at his stepfather and pointed. "This photo is the problem."

Victor re-examined the newspaper and then looked up at him. "The young lady in this one is okay, but not nearly as good-looking as that Matthews woman. She's smoking hot."

"Enough about her."

"Okay, okay," his stepfather said, still examining the photo. "You know, the old woman standing next to the young one in this picture looks kind of like…"

"A man in drag." Cole finished. He jabbed his finger toward the offending photo of an attractive young woman juxtaposed against an older one presumably representing Espresso. "Not only are they relegating us to the brand for senior citizens, they exaggerate the point with one of the ugliest old ladies I've ever seen."

"Well, as you just said, he's no lady."

A vein on the side of Cole's head pulsed. "You think?" Sarcasm permeated the question. "What gave it away, the hot mess of a gray wig or the damned goatee?"

"Hmm." Victor tilted his own graying head to one side, then the other as he continued to study the grainy color photo. "Not really a goatee. I'd say it was more of a five o'clock shadow."

"Are you actually defending that photo?" Cole asked.

The corner of his stepfather's mouth quirked upward.

"You know he kind of looks like the guy who stars in those Maw-Maw movies."

"Who or what is a Maw-Maw?"

Victor looked up, an incredulous look on his face. "Wow. You have been out of the country a long time. Maw-Maw is the star of a slew of movies about a wisecracking, busybody matriarch, who can't stop sticking her nose in her family's business." He chuckled and shook his head. "Can't believe you never heard of them. I have a couple on DVD. I'll let you borrow them."

"No, thank you," Cole said firmly, his patience waning.

"Oh, come on. You have to at least see *Maw-Maw Passes the Plate*. It's the one where Maw-Maw puts an envelope containing a thousand dollars into the church offering plate by mistake." His stepfather burst into a fit of laughter, slapping the newspaper against his thigh. "The old girl starts leaping over the church pews, like a sprinter clearing hurdles in the summer Olympics, trying to get it back. She even tackles a deacon. It's hilarious!"

Cole cleared his throat loudly.

"I'm not interested in any movie featuring a grown man wearing a dress. Right now, all I care about is this article and the damage it's doing to Espresso's image, which isn't one bit funny."

"Sorry about that, son." Victor dabbed at the tears that had gathered in his eyes from laughing. "I guess I got sidetracked." He extracted a pair of reading glasses from his shirt pocket and resumed studying the article.

A few minutes later, he shrugged. "Okay, so they took a bit of a dig at us. Try not to get so bent out of shape over it. It's not that big a deal."

"Not a big deal?" Cole fumed, the headline imprinted on his brain—Not Your Granny's Makeup: Stiletto Cosmetics Puts Its Spiked Heel in the Competition. He quoted the article, "As Cole Sinclair makes a last ditch attempt to rescue his family's declining Espresso Cosmetics from near extinction, an edgy new brand is poised to pick up the torch."

Victor removed his glasses, folded the paper and tucked it under his arm. "We just had our first successful collection in nearly a decade thanks to you," he said.

"And there wasn't a single word in the press about it, despite the efforts of our public relations team."

"Still, it was a huge boost to Espresso employees who haven't had much to celebrate in a very long time," the older man said. "You should be patting yourself on the back, not worrying about a ridiculous photo in some rag."

"*America Today* has a nationwide circulation. Not to mention online and international editions."

"My point is Espresso is finally making a comeback," Victor said.

"Comeback?" Cole leaned against the front of his desk and folded his arms. "We're a long way from what I'd consider a comeback.

"A sold-out holiday collection was a heck of a good start."

Cole shrugged off the praise with a grunt. His first order of business as CEO of Espresso's cosmetics division had been to sit down with the company's chief financial officer, Malcolm Doyle, to find out exactly where years of stagnant sales had left them financially.

The second had been to untie the hands of the creative and product-development teams and allow them to do their jobs. For too long their ideas had languished due to Victor's insistence on remaining loyal to what he believed Cole's mother would have wanted for her company.

"You've done more for Espresso in five months than I accomplished after years of being in charge." Victor's chin dropped to his chest, his gaze cast toward the carpet. "It's just I thought…"

"The success of the holiday collection was just a drop in the bucket." Cole cut him off, refusing to play the blame game.

All he cared about was making Espresso relevant in the cosmetics industry again. It was too late to take back the harsh words he'd exchanged with his mother the very last time he'd seen her. Now the only way he could make it up to her was to save her legacy.

He swallowed hard. "We'd need a tsunami to erase the red ink from the company books and our old-lady image from women's minds." Rounding his desk, Cole tapped at his computer keyboard until the survey he'd commissioned appeared on the screen. "I was going to email you a copy of this later, but you might as well take a look at it now."

Victor sat in Cole's leather executive chair, once again retrieving his reading glasses from his pocket.

"This is a survey taken over the holidays of customers shopping at various department-store cosmetics counters," Cole explained. He leaned over Victor's shoulder, right-clicking the mouse to expand a page. "Here are just a few of the comments female shoppers made when asked about Espresso."

The older man read aloud. "'My great-aunt uses their foundation. We call her Auntie Cake behind her back because her face always looks like it's been dipped in batter.'" Victor winced. "Ouch."

"It gets worse."

"You're kidding."

"Nope. Keep reading."

"'Their makeup counters are deader than a morgue.'"

Victor read another one. "'I didn't know they were still around.'"

Cole pointed out a remark made by a twenty-two-year-old woman actually making a purchase at an Espresso counter. This time he read it aloud. "'I'm only here because my grandmother ran out of her favorite pink lipstick. No way I'd wear this old-lady stuff. I'm a Stiletto girl all the way.'"

His stepfather exhaled a long drawn-out breath. "This is why you're so peeved about that article."

Cole nodded. "The more I think about it, the more I believe it's too late to change people's minds about us. Our senior-citizen image is too entrenched."

"But…" Victor started to protest, but Cole held up a hand to stop him.

"Hear me out," Cole said. "Why keep banging our heads against a brick wall? Stiletto already has the hip, edgy vibe and is gaining popularity with the young demographic we're chasing."

"I'm not following you, son."

Cole smiled for the first time in what felt like weeks. Why hadn't he thought of it before?

"It's the acquire-to-grow strategy—something I was in charge of implementing during my tenure at Force Cosmetics. Simply put, if we can't beat them, *we'll just have to buy them*."

He paused to give Victor a chance to let the idea sink in. "We would keep Stiletto's name and packaging the same, meanwhile continue to revamp Espresso and rebrand it as makeup for the classic or mature beauty or something along those lines."

The older man pressed his lips together a few moments, before he finally spoke. "Couldn't we just develop our own offshoot brand?"

Cole shrugged. "We could, but that would take a long

time. Even then, consumers can be fickle. There's no guarantee it would catch on and turn into a winner for us."

"But how?" Victor frowned, deepening the creases in his forehead. "You heard what Doyle said. The cosmetics division is buried in red ink. Your sister's Espresso Sanctuary spas propped us up until you came back and threw us a lifeline."

Cole crossed his arms over his chest. While Espresso's finances had dwindled in his absence, his personal wealth had grown tremendously. "Don't worry. I've got it covered," he said. "I'm about to make Ms. Matthews an offer too good to refuse."

Chapter 2

Sage Matthews pulled the phone away from her ear long enough to give it, and the woman on the other end of the line, the side eye.

"Your makeup brand would be a perfect addition to our store lineup."

The buyer for the trendy boutique chain droned on, but the silent alarms on Sage's bullshit detector drowned out the rest of her spiel. It sounded identical to the ones she'd heard all morning.

"Strange—that isn't what you said a few weeks ago." Sage kicked off her shoes under her desk and wiggled her toes. High heels were the worst form of torture, but when you owned a company called Stiletto, you had to dress the part.

She glanced at the notation she'd scribbled on a message slip next to the buyer's name. "I believe you said Stiletto's branding was too provocative. Your exact words were *downright raunchy*."

"Um…well," the woman stammered. "You must have misheard me. I said it was *delightfully racy* as in sexy. Clearly, there's been a misunderstanding."

Misunderstanding, huh? Sage stifled the harrumph on the tip of her tongue. "Hard to tell," she said, "considering the way your secretary tossed me out of your office afterward like she was a nightclub bouncer."

"Oh, dear. Please accept my apologies if my staff was a touch overzealous. Again, I assure you it was all a big mistake. One I hope we can…"

"Just stop." Sage had heard enough.

"P-pardon?"

"Before you continue, you should know I refuse to do business with anyone who lies to me."

Silence.

Figuring the buyer was weighing her options, Sage waited, making no attempt to fill the dead air. Long awkward moments passed, before a sigh emitted over the line. "Okay, the truth is I didn't want to risk offending my more conservative clientele by selling lipsticks and eyes shadows with names like Spank Me and Missionary Position."

There was another sigh, this one deeper and more drawn out. "Next thing I know, the hottest female singer on the planet is telling a national television audience she adores your lipsticks. Suddenly the same customers I was worried about offending are clamoring for Stiletto products, and I couldn't be more sorry for turning you down."

Finally, Sage thought, *the truth*.

She'd returned nearly a dozen calls that morning from eager buyers, the same people who had practically slammed the door in her face previously, criticizing everything from Stiletto's faux black leather packing to the titillating names of their products. Of course, they'd changed their tunes in the weeks since pop star Crave had whipped out a tube of Stiletto lipstick and called it her secret weapon.

Sage knew it was just foolish pride. Still, she couldn't help feel irked that instead of owning up to their blunder, they'd tried to gloss over it. Insulting her intelligence with meaningless flattery.

"My assistant will contact you later today to schedule a meeting to discuss adding Stiletto to your boutique's lineup," she said, satisfied. "However, you should know that as circumstances have changed, so has my first offer. Any deal we strike now will definitely have terms more favorable to Stiletto."

"Eh…uh…of course," the boutique's buyer said. "I look forward to our meeting."

Sage ended the call just as her assistant, Amelia, bounded into her office clutching a pink message slip. A huge grin deepened the dimples in the cheeks of her smooth brown skin. "I thought it would take forever for you to finally get off the phone."

"What's up?" Leaning forward in her office chair, Sage propped her elbows on her desktop. She dropped her chin to her chest and began rubbing out the kinks that had developed in her neck from talking on the phone all morning.

"You'll never guess who called for you." The nineteen-year-old shifted from one leg to the other, practically bouncing with excitement. "Not in a million years."

"Well, don't keep me…" Sage stopped midsentence and glanced up at her assistant. "Hold on. What are you still doing here?" She glanced at her watch. "Your accounting class starts in five minutes."

Amelia huffed and rolled her eyes toward the ceiling. "I know. I know."

The teen had started working for Stiletto a few hours a week after school during her last year of high school.

Sage thought she was doing the girl a favor, but quickly discovered that in the efficient and organized Amelia, she'd struck employee gold.

A year later, when graduation and her eighteenth birthday aged her out of the foster-care system, the job became full-time with the stipulation that Amelia would enroll in college. Having grown up in the foster-care system, Sage knew the importance of having an education to fall back on when you had no one to depend on but yourself.

"Well?" Sage raised a brow.

"But I couldn't leave. Not just yet. Not until I tell you who…"

"I don't care who called. There isn't anything or anyone more important than you being at school right now," Sage said.

The same brusque tone that sent her other employees, and most people, scurrying for cover rarely intimidated Amelia. Nor did it dampen her bubbly enthusiasm over the caller she was dying to tell her about.

"Stand down, General. I'm going to class, but first you have to hear who called you before I explode."

"For goodness' sake. Spit it out so you can haul your fanny over to the community college." Sage sighed. "And if you're going to call me General, can't you do it behind my back like everyone else around here?"

"Cole Sinclair!" The name popped out of her assistant's mouth like the cork on a bottle of champagne.

Sage studied the message slip Amelia handed her and tried to place the familiar name. Then it hit her. "As in Espresso Cosmetics?" He and his family's company had been a footnote in a feature article on Stiletto that had run a few days ago in *America Today*.

"Well, yeah, but Cole Sinclair is worth way more than that granny makeup company he runs." Amelia dismissed the connection with a flick of her hand. "Remember the puzzle game we deleted from our phones and you banned from our office computers because it was too addictive?"

Sage nodded, recalling getting so caught up in the colorful game she'd spent an entire evening matching trios of circus clowns in an attempt to beat enough levels to earn the elusive title of ultimate ringmaster.

"Well, Cole Sinclair invested in the gaming studio that developed it years ago, back when it was just two college kids in their parents' basement. His meager investment turned him into a millionaire twenty times over when the business eventually sold to a major corporation," Amelia said. "It was one of the topics in my entrepreneurship class last semester."

While the background information on Sinclair was mildly interesting, Sage's concern was her own business and turning it into a multimillion-dollar endeavor. She stared at the name on the message slip. "Did he say what he wanted?"

"Only that it was important," Amelia said. "What do you think?"

Sage shrugged. "Maybe he's miffed about that article in *America Today*. The mention of Espresso wasn't exactly flattering. Nor was that photo of the young, chic woman symbolizing us versus the old one that was supposedly Espresso."

"Or maybe—" Amelia paused dramatically "—maybe he took one look at the photo of you with that article and fell head over heels for you. And he wants to ask you out on a date. Just think about it." The young woman let out a squeal. "A tall, good-looking millionaire is smitten by your photo, falls hopelessly in love and is determined to sweep you off your feet."

Sage stared at the dreamy look on the teen's face, unable

to believe the crap coming out of her mouth. How could a girl so smart about most things be so dumb about this one? Sage waited a beat, reaching for diplomatic words to set her assistant straight without hurting her feelings.

There were none.

"That is the stupidest thing I've ever heard," she said.

"It could happen," Amelia protested.

"Yeah, and maybe he'll charge into my office on a white horse wearing a suit of armor or bare chested like the men on the covers of those ridiculous romance novels you've always got your nose stuck in."

This time it was her assistant who frowned. "There's nothing wrong with being a romantic. In fact, the more I think about it, a date is just what you need. It would loosen you up, and maybe folks around here might stop calling you General behind your back."

They could call her Godzilla for all she cared, as long as they did their jobs—and did them well. "You need to spend more time with your textbooks and less reading those silly romances." Sage checked her watch.

"I'm going, but first I need to schedule your meeting with Mr. Sinclair."

Amelia pulled the smartphone she used for work from her pants pocket. "He wants to see you at your earliest convenience." She tapped on the screen with a stylus she'd retrieved from behind her ear. "Your schedule is packed, but I could bump one of your other appointments so you can see him later this afternoon or perhaps first thing to-morrow."

Sage held up a finger. "I haven't decided if I'm meeting with him at all."

The younger woman looked up from the phone. "You're joking, right?"

"You, better than anyone, know I rarely joke."

"Aren't you curious? I can hardly wait to find out what he wants."

Sage fixed her assistant with her most intimidating, no-nonsense glare. "You'll have to wait because you're leaving for your accounting class *right now.*"

Grumbling, the young woman reluctantly did as she was told.

Sage had no idea why Cole Sinclair had called. But unlike Amelia, she didn't indulge in far-fetched fantasies. Sage lived in the real world.

And in the real world, when rich people wanted to talk business, they wanted to trick poor people out of something valuable.

Chapter 3

Money might not buy happiness, but Cole knew enough of it would buy just about everything else.

It was the reason he walked the short blocks from the Espresso building to the downtown restaurant he'd selected for his meeting with Sage Matthews, confident he'd be the new owner of Stiletto Cosmetics when he returned.

Cole was also intrigued.

The woman had actually put him off for over a week. A humorless chuckle pushed through his lips, leaving a vapor trail as his warm breath hit the January air.

No one put him on the back burner. *Not anymore*, Cole thought. When he snapped his fingers, people jumped. Especially women.

Another side effect of deep pockets.

So either Ms. Matthews had somehow missed the articles written about him by reporters obsessed with his bank balance, or she was one of the few people who simply didn't care.

A blast of heat hit him as he pulled open the restaurant door and strode inside. Immediately, he saw a woman with her back to him talking to the hostess.

Her big, bold hair and long, shapely legs left no doubt about her identity. Shiny, patent leather boots hugged her calves, and she wore a red wool coat with a thigh-grazing hemline just shy of indecent.

Cole felt the corner of his mouth tic upward into a reluctant smile as his stepfather's words popped into his head: *not a thing here that would put a frown on a man's face.*

He overheard the hostess, who hadn't seen him come in. "Mr. Sinclair hasn't arrived yet, but let me take your coat, and I'll show you to the table he reserved in our private dining room."

"No, thanks." Cole watched Sage Matthews consult a plain wristwatch with a worn, black strap, a feminine version of his own. "We're supposed to meet here in five minutes. If he's not on time, I'm leaving."

"Mr. Sinclair is always punctual," the hostess offered.

The woman in the short coat and high-heeled boots bobbed her head in a curt nod. "If he wants to see me, he'd better be."

Cole cleared his throat, the gesture commanding the attention of both women. "I'm here—" he glanced at his own Timex and then pointedly at Ms. Matthews "—with four minutes to spare."

She met his gaze, not a trace of sheepishness at being overheard in her expression. If anything, challenge flickered in her chocolate-brown eyes. "Good. Time is money, Mr. Sinclair. Mine is valuable."

Cole blinked. The statement was something he'd usually say, and she'd delivered it just like he would have— blunt and to the point. "Well, let's not waste either of ours standing here," he said.

Within minutes, the hostess had taken their coats, and escorted them through the bustling dining room to a stair-case leading to the private room he liked to use when conducting business outside the Espresso building. As they walked Cole couldn't help notice the statuesque woman with the riot of kinky curls move through the upscale restaurant as if she owned it, garnering appreciative glances from every man in the room.

Including him.

However, this lunch had an agenda and nothing would distract him from it. Not even a sweet pair of legs, show-cased by a minidress and fantasy-inducing shiny stiletto boots.

A waiter appeared with menus immediately after they were seated. He took their drink orders and disappeared to retrieve them.

"Thank you for agreeing to meet with me, Ms. Mat-thews." Cole didn't bother opening the menu. The en-trées were the standard fare of most upscale restaurants. A minuscule serving of meat or fish smothered in creams and vegetables pureed beyond recognition and served on a plate that appeared destined for an art museum rather than someone's stomach.

However, this restaurant was currently the hot ticket in town for fine dining, and it made the right impression at lunch and dinner business meetings in an industry where image was everything.

Cole's personal preference would have been to conduct business over real food—a burger, barbecue sandwich or a slice of pizza. One of which he'd probably grab after-ward to celebrate his having reached a verbal agreement with Ms. Matthews.

He glanced across the table at his lunch companion, who was perusing the menu. Again, she surprised him.

Most people would have rushed to fill the silence with small talk by now.

His gaze dropped to her lips, painted the same bold, sassy red as her dress. The firm line she held them in didn't distract from their fullness.

She looked up, and her eyes locked with his. Caught staring, Cole didn't divert his bold appraisal.

"I was checking out your lipstick shade," he said, making it clear both to her, and to himself, that any interest in her mouth was purely professional.

"It's one of Stiletto's bestsellers." She lifted a perfectly arched brow. "It's called Badass."

Cole licked his own lips, his mouth suddenly dry. *I'll just bet you are.*

The errant thought popped into his head so quickly, he feared he'd said it aloud. Her impassive expression assured him he hadn't, and he exhaled in relief.

The waiter reappeared with their drinks. Cole used the moments it took for them to order two of the chef's specialties to give himself a mental knock upside the head.

Stay on task, man, he silently warned. *This is a business meeting, not a date.* He reached for his water glass and took a long sip. No more getting sidetracked by shiny stiletto boots or impossibly red lips.

"Now how about you tell me what's on your mind, Mr. Sinclair?"

Cole swallowed, the question immediately shutting down illicit images of her full red lips pressed against his and those badass boot-encased legs wrapped firmly around his waist.

"Excuse me?" The words came out like a frog's croak.

"Since we've established neither of us likes to waste time," she said. "I assumed we could skip the preliminaries and get right to the reason for my being here."

An odd sense of déjà vu passed over him. How many times had he said the exact same thing? *Plenty*, Cole silently answered his own question.

If he didn't know better, he'd think he was sitting across the table from a female version of himself.

Nah, couldn't be, he thought.

Leaning forward, Cole crossed his arms on the table. "I want to buy Stiletto."

Her eyes widened, his only clue he'd caught her off guard. She recovered quickly, and then she, too, leaned forward in her chair and crossed her arms on the table.

"Then this meeting truly was a waste of time for both of us, Mr. Sinclair, because my company isn't for sale."

That's what you think, Cole thought. "Don't be too hasty, Ms. Matthews," he said aloud. The easy Southern drawl he'd thought he'd lost in Europe permeated his warning. "After all, you don't know what I'm offering."

"Doesn't matter."

"Oh, I think it will."

"Well, let's hear it."

Her tone taunted him with an unspoken challenge. Cole could hardly wait to see her expression when he not only met her expectations, but surpassed them.

Eye to eye, neither of their stares wavered. Nor did Cole's confidence that he'd leave here with what he wanted. Reaching into the inside pocket of his suit jacket, he pulled out a folded scrap of paper and slid it across the white linen tablecloth.

Her fingertips grazed his as she took it, sending an almost audible crackle of electricity through him. He scoured her expression for an indication she'd felt it, too. For the first time since they'd met, she diverted her eyes.

She'd felt it all right.

Abruptly snatching her hand back, she took the slip of

paper. His own hand still tingling in the spot where they'd inadvertently touched, Cole watched her square her shoulders. Her back stiffened as she straightened in her chair.

"It doesn't matter what amount you've written. I've already told you, Stiletto isn't for sale."

Cole simply inclined his head toward the slip of paper. He stared at her fingernails, painted the same bold red as her lips, while she opened it.

This time, Sage Matthews couldn't disguise her reaction. The paper fell from her hands on the table, and that delectable red mouth dropped open. A stuttering sound came out of it.

"O-oh, my God." She covered a gasp with her hand and stared up him. "You're joking, right?"

"I never joke about business, Ms. Matthews." Satisfaction and a sense of imminent victory flooded him. The taste was so sweet, he'd probably forgo dessert.

Cole picked up the paper bearing his offer and placed it back in her hand. She was still examining it when the waiter returned with their entrées.

"Why don't you just let that figure sink in while we enjoy lunch?" Cole did his best not to sound smug. "We can discuss it after we eat."

The woman recovered quickly, her surprise replaced with a mask of indifference. But Cole knew better.

"Fine by me." She refolded the paper and put it aside.

Cole switched focus to his food. He'd originally planned to go out for a simpler meal later; however, his impending triumph had given him quite an appetite. He'd just have to make do with the chef's specialty, an overdressed piece of fish so fancy it deserved its own art exhibit.

He reached for his fork, but the frown on his dining companion's face as she looked at her food stopped him. "Everything all right?"

She wrinkled her nose, and for the first time he noticed the faint smattering of freckles dotting it. "Honestly?" she asked.

Cole chuckled. "Somehow I don't think you know how to be any other way."

"I realize you're accustomed to sitting down to a so-called gastronomical experience at every meal, but I'm a simple country girl with simple tastes. I'd have been fine with a pulled pork sandwich or burger."

"Unbelievable," Cole murmured. *More like amazing.*

She held up a hand. "Don't go getting offended on me. It's just a personal preference." She picked up her fork and poked what appeared to be pureed spinach. "I'm sure whatever is under all this froufrou garnishing tastes just fine."

Cole threw his head back and laughed. Too bad this wasn't a date because Sage Matthews was almost too good to be true. If he wasn't careful, he could end up liking her...*a lot.* "First of all, from what I see there's nothing simple about you," he said. "Second, you and I have the exact same opinion when it comes to food."

"Really?" She brightened and a smile touched her lips.

He nodded, and then scanned the surroundings. "Write-ups in *Bon Appétit* and *Saveur* magazines have made this place a hot ticket. It impresses the people I do business with who love both its exclusivity and the cuisine." Cole shrugged. "But me? I'll take cheeseburger with a side of onion rings over froufrou every time."

"My absolute favorite meal," she said. "Thanks to an electronic billboard I pass on the way to work advertising a new burger place in town, I've been giving in to a craving for it every day for the past week for both lunch and dinner."

"Burger Tower?"

She nodded. "Have you eaten there yet?"

"I haven't had the opportunity; however, I can see the very same billboard from my office window. It leaves me practically drooling."

She leaned in conspiratorially, her brown eyes sparkling with mischief. "Well, Mr. Sinclair, from one burger lover to another, they're positively addictive."

Cole rarely acted on impulse, but Sage Matthews was such a refreshing change of pace. She didn't pander to him with her eyes on his wallet for what she could get. She impressed him as a woman who spoke her mind and didn't give a damn what he or anyone else thought about it.

He was well aware he'd asked her here for purely professional reasons. Still, he found himself wanting to see her again.

"Call me Cole," he said. "Because once we conclude our business, I'd like to take you out for one of those burgers. Feed both you and your addiction."

She blinked. "As in a date?"

His common sense told him this wasn't the time or place. Intermingling the personal and professional broke the most basic rule of business. A rule he'd never been tempted to bend until now.

He knew better.

Cole couldn't defend his actions. Nor could he stop himself from telling her exactly what was on his mind.

"You couldn't have missed it. I'm not even sure what to call it—an air of familiarity?" He searched for the right words to describe the coincidences, but came up empty and hoped he didn't sound like a fool.

"It's almost like looking in a mirror," she said, softly.

Cole exhaled, and then nodded.

"Not physically, of course," she quickly added. "But we do appear to have an awful lot in common."

"More than that…" Again, he found himself reaching

for just the right words, not wanting to make presumptions or come on too strong.

Her gaze dropped to his hand. The same one her touch had left tingling. "I felt it, too."

"It's the reason why I'm asking you on a date in the middle of a business lunch. I'd like an opportunity to get to know you better."

The sparkle in her eyes dimmed. "As much as I'd enjoy that, I don't think it's going happen."

"Why not? Are you involved with someone?" Of course, she was, Cole thought. He hadn't seen a ring on her finger, but that didn't mean anything."

"No, I'm not seeing anyone. Honestly, you're the first man I've met in a long time who's piqued my interest."

"Then what's the problem?"

"Oh, I'm not the one with the problem," she said. "You'll be, once I turn down your offer to buy Stiletto."

"Are you sure you want to do that?"

His voice was velvet smooth. Its deep, melodic cadence threw Sage off her game. She didn't think she'd had it in her to act like Amelia. Yet, for a while she'd let herself be lured into entertaining the ludicrous notions of instant attraction and serendipity.

Get a grip, she silently scolded. It was just one touch and a few coincidences.

Her guard firmly back into place, Sage needed to make her position clear. Before Cole Sinclair talked her out of her company and her panties.

"I've made my decision," she said. "No sale."

Cole raised a brow. "Maybe I haven't explained that the figure I gave you is merely a starting point," he said. "One I'm willing to sweeten with a few more zeros."

Sage swallowed, hard. The offer was already beyond

generous, and at this point, much more than her company was worth. *If* money was the only measuring stick.

The massive figure didn't take the intangibles into account. She didn't have family and had sacrificed the few friends and relationships she'd had by putting all her time and effort into her small company.

While Stiletto was simply a commodity to a man like Cole Sinclair, something easily bought or sold, it was her everything.

He leaned back in his seat and crossed his arms over his broad chest. "Think about it, Ms. Matthews," he continued. "We're talking about a lot of money here. You're a young woman. Wisely invested, it'll last a lifetime. You could travel the world worry- and responsibility-free."

"And how did that work for you?"

Sage caught the tic of a muscle beneath the shadow of beard along his strong jawline. The tiny telltale movement was the only indication her question made him uncomfortable. "You spent the past few years on your boat sailing around—where was it I read, again?—Italy? Greece?"

"Both."

"Yet, instead of continuing to enjoy the idyllic carefree life you described, you're back in Nashville running Espresso." She leaned back in her chair and crossed her arms over her chest. She noticed her unconscious movements mirrored his and abruptly unfolded her arms. "Not only that, you want my company, too."

"I came back home because my family needed me. The company my mother poured her lifeblood into needs me."

"Then you should understand why I won't sell Stiletto," she said. "I've spent years building this business. Now that it's finally showing some promise, you want me to just hand it over to you."

"Sell it to me, Ms. Matthews, for what we both know is triple what your small company is actually worth."

His statement brought up a question that had niggled at her since she'd seen his staggering starting offer.

"I'm curious. Why are you willing to pay big money for my 'small company'?"

Their waiter returned. A slight incline of Cole's head and he quickly removed the plates of barely touched food, then vanished as if he'd never entered the room.

Sage met the hard stare of that man across the table. She held it through a tension-filled silence, wondering if he'd give her the real answer to her question or some pat bullshit reply.

Part of her hoped he'd do the latter. It would make it easier to dismiss Cole Sinclair and snuff out any attraction she felt toward him.

"Our image problem is no secret. The article that ran in *America Today* certainly didn't help it," he said. "Acquiring Stiletto would give Espresso instant access to and credibility with a younger market, which we desperately need."

Sage shouldn't have been surprised. Everything about him so far had been straightforward. The stark honesty in his reply raised him in her esteem.

Despite her efforts to the contrary, she found herself actually liking Cole Sinclair, though not enough to sell him her company.

"While I understand your predicament, you'll have to find another solution to Espresso's problems. Stiletto isn't for sale. Not at any price."

"So you've said." He seemed nonplussed at her declaration.

However, Sage knew he wasn't ready to give up, because they seemed to be two of a kind, and in his shoes, she wouldn't.

"Be smart, Ms. Matthews. Not only is this a once-in-a-lifetime opportunity for you, it's one for your company, too," he said. "And while I applaud what you've been able to accomplish with Stiletto with such limited resources, I think you've hit a ceiling. You won't be able to take it to the next level."

And just like that, Sage didn't like him so much anymore.

"But you can?"

"Yes," he said, matter-of-factly. The lack of conceit in his tone irked her more than his words.

Sage snorted. "With what, money?"

"Money, along with two other things you don't have—infrastructure and experience."

Sage listened as he continued to build his case.

"Espresso may have an image problem, but it also has the distribution channels. We have the department store counter space and Espresso Sanctuary spas."

"Thanks to that mention from Crave, Stiletto is on a roll," Sage countered. "It's only a matter of time before I'll have those things, too."

Cole chuckled as if she'd told him a knock-knock joke. The deep, rich sound sent the same involuntary tingles through her body as his touch, and at the same time, ratcheted up her annoyance. "Perhaps in ten years or so," he said. "I can do it now."

Sage grudgingly acknowledged the man had a point, but only to herself. She'd never give him the satisfaction of saying it aloud.

"Like you said, I'm a young woman. Time is on my side." She spared a glance at the folded slip of paper with his offer, before leveling her gaze at him. "Besides, there's more to taking a business to the next level than deep pockets."

"Deep pockets and *experience*."

"Experience in what?" Sage muttered. "Lucky investments? Globetrotting?"

Annoyance flashed in his dark brown eyes as they bored into hers, but he extinguished the show of emotion as quickly as it sparked.

He exhaled a long drawn-out sigh. "I grew up in this industry at my mother's side." He spoke slowly as if he were correcting a naughty child. "During my hiatus from Espresso, I indeed made a shrewd investment that paid off royally, which gave me an opportunity to take off and see a bit of the world. However, I also spent seven of those nine years working my way up the ladder to vice president of acquisitions at Force Cosmetics."

Sage's mouth dropped open at his disclosure, and she promptly slammed it shut, hoping he hadn't noticed.

"The articles written about me tend to leave out that particular part of my bio, preferring to focus on my so-called lucky investment," he said.

Damn. An internet search on Cole Sinclair had pulled up at least a dozen articles. None of them had mentioned he'd had a top job at Force. They practically dominated the beauty industry.

Also, it seemed strange.

Why had he gone to work for an international giant like Force Cosmetics when he had blood ties to Espresso, she wondered. Sage shrugged off the question. It wasn't any of her business.

"Don't underestimate me, Ms. Matthews," he said. "There's a lot more to me than money."

"I'll keep that in mind." Sage conceded the round of verbal sparring to him. Still, it wouldn't get him what he wanted.

He rested his back against the chair. His easy smile

returned, oozing with Southern charm, but his dark eyes brimmed with an unspoken challenge.

"Also, don't let pride stand in the way of your common sense." Like his smile, the deep, melodic baritone belied the man's uncompromising words. "Let me take Stiletto off your hands because the bottom line is I can run your company better than you ever could."

Sage stood abruptly. The condescension and the kernel of truth in his hard-hitting statement stung as if he'd pelted her with a handful of rocks.

"This meeting is over, Mr. Sinclair," she said, walking toward the door of the private dining room.

Sage didn't intend to give him a backward glance but turned around at the sound of that arrogant, infuriating, *panty-melting* voice.

"Keep in mind, if you won't sell Stiletto to me, I'll be forced to go with my alternative plan. One I don't think you'll like."

Sage's eyes narrowed as she glared at him. Sitting there, surrounded by an air of confident cool, as though he didn't have a care in the world. "I have two words for you and your granny-makeup company, Mr. Sinclair. *Bring it.*"

"How about we get on a first name basis, Sage?" The smile never left his face. "Because I intend to bring it all right. I just hope you can handle it."

Chapter 4

Cole walked briskly through the streets leading back to the Espresso building.

Bring it!

The taunt echoed through his head, leaving him unable to determine if the vapor emitted by his body was generated by his breath colliding with the cold or the steam venting from his ears.

Not only did the stubborn woman dismiss his perfectly reasonable argument. She'd tossed an extremely generous offer back in his face.

Who turns their nose up at that kind of money?

"Sage Matthews, that's who," Cole grumbled aloud, oblivious to passersby making a wide berth around the man talking to himself.

Images of big hair, shiny black boots and tempting red-slicked lips bombarded him as he yanked open the lobby door of the Espresso building.

The once-modern concrete-and-steel structure, built by

his late uncle, had been a tremendous source of pride to his mother when it was erected thirty years ago. Now the eleven-story building stood half-empty, dwarfed by dozens of gleaming new towers dominating the Nashville skyline.

Cole sighed. Though they'd worked through most of their differences, the building continued to be a sticking point in his and Victor's relationship. Cole and his sisters had agreed selling it was their best option, but his stepfather wouldn't hear of it.

They could have easily outvoted him months ago. However, Cole thought the older man needed more time to accept the inevitable.

It was just as well, he thought. Right now he needed to focus on convincing the infuriatingly sexy Sage Matthews to give him what he wanted.

Her company.

Acknowledging both the security guard and reception desk with a nod, he strode across the lobby's marble floor to the elevators. Fortunately, two of the three elevators in the older building were working today.

This should have been a chip shot, he thought, as the elevator whisked him up to the executive floor. He'd expected to be talking with his lawyers by now, instructing them to prepare the paperwork sealing the deal. Only there was no deal.

And nothing had gone as he'd expected.

The elevator chimed and the doors opened on the eleventh floor. Cole pushed open the door to the outer office of the executive suite. He was relieved to see Victor's door closed. Cole wasn't looking forward to filling his stepfather in on the details of the disastrous meeting.

Or your totally unprofessional behavior.

Cole shook his head. He'd actually asked her out on a date. It was unlike him to be so impulsive or stupid.

Then again, he'd never felt so in sync with a woman. Sage Matthews had been right about one thing, when it came to their personalities and mannerisms, it was indeed like looking in the mirror.

"Is that frown tattooed on your face or do you wear it just for me?" The gravelly ex-smoker's voice of the secretary he shared with his stepfather broke into his thoughts.

Cole groaned inwardly, pausing at the large desk in the office bridging his and Victor's offices.

The way his day had been going today, it figured Loretta Walker would be faithfully manning her station instead of taking a long lunch when the boss was away like the secretaries and administrative assistants he'd had in the past. Cole fixed the silver-haired sexagenarian with a glare that would have sent any other Espresso employee fleeing to the opposite side of the building.

The woman didn't so much as flinch.

"This is my special face just for you," he said. "I laugh like the Tickle Me Elmo doll for everyone else."

"Lucky me. I get to spend my workdays looking at that sour mug." She handed him a few opened envelopes from the stack of the day's mail. "These require your attention. I'll handle the rest."

"You're welcome to retire anytime," Cole said as he sifted through them.

"No can do," Loretta said. "I've got a granddaughter to get through medical school, remember?"

"Then how about a paid vacation, somewhere far, far away?"

"Vacation?" Loretta threw her head back and laughed, the raspy sound filling the office that had been her domain for nearly three decades. "I can barely take a bathroom break without everything around here falling apart. Face it, I'm both indispensable and irreplaceable."

Despite his bluster, Cole couldn't refute it. Loretta was also smart, paid attention to detail and took no crap whatsoever from him, or the members of his family that bore the name Gray, including the late Selina Sinclair Gray.

As a kid, he'd once asked his mother why she let an employee get away with the kind of backtalk she'd never tolerate from her children or anyone else.

She'd told him Loretta was more than just a secretary. She explained Loretta kept the office operating with clockwork precision, which gave her the freedom to focus on running Espresso.

"More importantly, Loretta calls it like she sees it, and possesses the courage to speak her mind regardless of the consequences," his mother had said. "Everybody should have someone like her in their life."

At the time, Cole had believed his mother the wisest person he'd ever known. All her big decisions had been good ones, right up until her last one, which still confounded him.

He forced back the hard feelings that had separated him from his family for years. His thoughts drifted back to the woman he'd met this afternoon.

Sage Matthews hadn't had a problem speaking her mind, either.

Their short meeting had taken him through a gamut of emotions. He couldn't remember the last time he'd been so intrigued, irritated or challenged, and he had to admit, totally turned on.

"Is that a tic or did you actually just crack a smile?"

"Tic," Cole answered automatically, "brought on by a certain exasperating secretary." Although, he knew a smile brought on by the recent memory of a certain woman in red had indeed touched his lips.

Loretta grunted. "If you're all done twitching, mind

telling me what time you want your lawyers here to hammer out the details of the Stiletto deal?"

The next grunt that sounded in the outer office came from him. His lips tightened. Any hint of a smile connected to his lunchtime encounter vanished, replaced with the last emotion his lunch companion had left him with—annoyance.

"Well?" Loretta pressed.

"There is no Stiletto deal." Cole admitted, then quickly amended. "Yet."

The long-time secretary's hoarse cackle filled his ears. All she needed to complete the effect was a chalkboard to scratch her nails across. "Gave you hell, didn't she?"

Although he'd never admit it aloud, Sage Matthews certainly had.

"Good for her, bringing you down a peg or two," Loretta continued. Her gravelly voice trailed him into his office. "It's about time you met your match."

Cole closed the door firmly behind him. However, his secretary's parting shot lingered. He couldn't deny the similarities between them, but his *match*? Ms. Matthews had a long way to go before she possessed the capability to bring him down a peg.

Walking over to the window, he shoved his hands into his pants pockets. He stared blankly at the flashing billboard in the distance and plotted his next move.

"I can't believe you walked out on Cole Sinclair."

Sage rose from her chair, braced her palms on her desktop and leaned forward. Had Amelia lost her mind? "Did you not hear a word I just said? The man threatened to come after Stiletto."

"Well…" Her assistant hedged, tilting her head to one side.

"Well, what?" Sage snapped. She fisted her hands on

her hips waiting to hear what possible explanation the young woman could conjure up to justify the man's insufferable behavior.

"You did tell him to 'bring it,'" Amelia said. "And knowing you as I do, I'm sure it was more like a barked command."

"Me?" Sage asked incredulously. Her knuckles dug deeper into her sides. "All I did was show up for a lunch meeting, which I should add, *you* wouldn't give me a moment's peace about until I agreed to go."

Her assistant held her hands up. "Hold on, General," she said. "I certainly didn't mean for you to march downtown and purposely provoke him."

Sage plopped down in her office chair and crossed her arms over her chest. "He was the one provoking me."

"You aren't one of the richest people in town."

"Please, don't mention money." Sage rolled her eyes toward the beams and pipes stretching across the ceiling of the former factory that housed Stiletto's headquarters as well as several other businesses. "He was tossing out dollars like a freak in a strip club."

Amelia laughed and then stopped abruptly. She narrowed her eyes. "So exactly how much was his offer to buy Stiletto?"

"That would fall under the category of none of your business."

"How about a ballpark figure?" The teen shrugged. "You turned him down anyway. What difference does it make?"

Sage thought it over a moment. It wasn't as if Amelia would spread it around the office. She could be a loopy romantic, but she was as discreet as she was efficient.

"Let's just say it was a couple of ballparks."

"And you didn't take the deal?"

"Of course, not. Stiletto isn't for sale," Sage said. "And you weren't there. He was condescending and…" Her voice trailed off as the sound of his easy baritone came back to her. Deep, rich and melodic. It made her want him to eat dessert in bed with him, *naked*.

"And what?" Amelia raised a brow.

"H-he was just so smug," Sage stammered over the words.

A slow smile spread over her assistant's lips. "And what else?"

"O-overbearing, insufferable, overconfident…" Again, her reaction to him at lunch waylaid her train of thought, and she automatically rubbed the spot where their hands had accidentally brushed.

"Interesting." The young woman's eyes widened as if she'd just been told a secret, and the smile on her face morphed into a full-fledged grin. "He sounds an awful lot like someone else I know."

"What are you grinning at?" Sage snapped. "Stop it."

Instead, Amelia narrowed her gaze. She made a few *hmm* and *mmm* sounds as she looked her up and down.

Sage squirmed uncomfortably in her chair. "What on earth is the matter with you?"

The young woman ignored the question, continuing her examination. "Cheeks flushed. Eyes glazed over. You're practically glowing," she said, making Sage feel as though she was in a doctor's office instead of her own. "And notice how you were all breathless and stammering when you talked about Mr. Sinclair."

Amelia nodded her head knowingly as if she already had the answer to her own question. "Not in a million years did I think I'd be saying this to you, but you look exactly like a smitten heroine in one of my romance novels."

Although she was immune to them, Sage gave her assistant a laser-beam side eye. "I'm acting insulted and extremely annoyed…because I am."

However, Sage didn't know who she was more pissed at, the man with the bedroom voice who believed he could run her business better than she, or herself for even having considered a date with him.

"If you say so."

"I do say so," Sage insisted, remembering his last words to her and the excessive confidence with which he'd delivered them.

I intend to bring it all right. I just hope you can handle it.

His declaration had come off as a double entendre. She'd caught both the all-business challenge and the sensual promise. Sage only wished there was a way for her to show him he'd taunted the wrong woman and wipe the smug smile off his handsome face.

Oblivious, Amelia exhaled a dreamy sigh filled with youthful naïveté. "I think Mr. Sinclair made quite the impression on you."

Sage's stomach growled, reminding her she still hadn't had lunch. "He made me so mad, I didn't even eat…"

The words died on her lips as an idea hit her.

Not just an idea, a maneuver so outrageous it would make Cole Sinclair think twice about underestimating her again. *But you couldn't*, she thought. *You wouldn't dare go through with it.*

Oh, yes, I would.

Her assistant waved a hand in front of her face, and Sage blinked. "You haven't heard a word I've said. I was trying to tell you…" Amelia paused, then frowned. "Uh-oh. What's going on in that head of yours?"

Sage feigned cluelessness. "Whatever do you mean?"

"It looks like you just sprouted devil horns on your head. The only thing missing is the diabolical laugh."

Her decision made, Sage slapped her palms against her desk and stood. Time to rally the troops. "I want you to add fifty additional beauty bloggers to the invitation list for our Valentine's Day's event," she said. "We're going to make it even bigger and even better."

"Will do."

She watched her assistant make the notation. "Then send Joe Archer from advertising into my office. I've got a job for him," Sage said. "I'm about to teach Mr. Sinclair a lesson he won't soon forget."

Amelia shook her head. "Sounds like you've already made him angry. I really don't think you should provoke him any further."

"Never mind what you think. Just get Archer in here."

Her assistant heaved an exaggerated sigh. "All right, I'll do as you ordered, General. I just hope you don't start the battle of the Nashville cosmetic companies."

So what if she did? Sage thought. The man had made it clear he intended to bring it. She was simply firing the first salvo, because the best defense was a good offense.

Her only regret was that she wouldn't be there to see the look on Sinclair's face.

Chapter 5

A week after their disastrous lunch, Sage Matthews remained on Cole's mind. His thoughts bounced from those sexy, shapely legs to that sassy mouth of hers painted the hottest shade of red he'd ever seen.

"Mr. Sinclair?"

Cole blinked, the sound of his name dragging him back to reality. Damn, he'd done it again.

And again, he told himself he was only pondering his next step to persuade the woman to sell her business.

"Sorry, could you repeat that?" Cole glanced around the coffee- and croissant-laden conference-room table where Espresso's department heads had gathered that morning for their biweekly meeting. His uncharacteristic distracted behavior drew a quizzical stare from Victor and a smug, know-it-all one from Loretta, who had been needling him all week about Stiletto's owner rejecting his offer.

He looked past them to the company's special events coordinator.

Tammy Barnes adjusted her eyeglasses. "I was saying it appears the Valentine's Day minimakeover event at our department store counters will have some competition, at least locally," she said. "Stiletto Cosmetics is holding an event the same afternoon."

Preston Tate's buttons strained to keep his shirt closed as he hurriedly washed down his third croissant with a gulp of coffee. "So we anticipate a lower-than-expected turnout," Tate, who was the head of their marketing team, chimed in. "It'll also mean generating less buzz nationwide, when the bloggers take to social media with comments and photos all about Stiletto."

As Cole listened, he wondered if this event was Sage's idea of getting back at him. She'd been furious when she'd stormed out of the restaurant. Moreover, the woman had practically challenged him. *Just like you did to her.*

Seated at his right, Loretta glanced down at her tablet computer. She'd balked when he'd upgraded every Espresso employee to the latest technology upon his return. Now the tablet rarely left her hands.

"Next on the agenda is Lola," she said.

A collective groan echoed across the room at the mention of Cole's youngest sister, and a young man seated at the opposite end of the conference table cleared his throat. "A few days ago, she and some of her model friends held a wild party in London and totally trashed their hotel suite. Now the European tabloids are having a field day. I think we need to…"

"Nonsense." Victor cut him off. "You can't believe anything the media reports anyway."

"But they had photos, and considering Lola is the face of Espresso, it reflects badly on the company," the young man countered.

"Brat," Loretta grunted.

"Watch your mouths. That's my baby girl you're talking about," Victor warned. "Those damn tabloids are making a big deal out of nothing. End of story. Case closed."

The faces around the table turned to Cole, knowing he was the one with the final word on any subject concerning the company. "I agree with Victor," he said. "Lola's just high-spirited."

"Enabler." Loretta snorted.

Cole held up a silencing hand and then turned his attention back to their marketing head. "Tate, I want to hear more about this event of Stiletto's."

"I'll just bet you do," Loretta muttered under her breath.

Cole shot his secretary a censorious glare, which earned him another gravelly snort. If she were anyone else, she would have been looking for a new job.

"It's a meet and greet for social media beauty gurus," Preston said. "Light refreshments, swag bags, et cetera."

Cole tapped his fingertip against the table. "Do you happen to know if this was something they pulled together in the past week?"

"I don't think so." Preston shrugged. "Looks like they posted it on their website a month ago."

Cole nodded absently. He was just being paranoid, he reasoned. Sage might be bold. The name of her lip color crossed his mind. However, she wasn't badass enough to take him on...or was she?

A thump vibrated the conference table, jolting him out of his reverie.

"Dang it!" Victor stood abruptly, drawing concerned stares from the room. He stomped his foot. "Leg fell asleep."

The older man shook his leg. He walked over to the wall of windows, on the other side of the room to coax life back into his sluggish limb. Located two floors below Cole's office, the floor-to-ceiling windows offered the same pan-oramic view, but at a lower vantage point.

"Funny you should ask about last week, though." Preston swiped at his tablet. "It looks as though they expanded the event a week ago and reached out to more bloggers and YouTube vloggers."

Maybe he wasn't being paranoid after all, Cole thought. Was this Sage's way of taking him on? He dismissed the idea. The challenge she'd issued had simply been an angry rant. Nothing more.

Tammy raised her hand to get their attention before clearing her throat. "Does anyone know when Tia will be back? I need to talk to her about including the spas in an upcoming event."

Cole shrugged. His sister and brother-in-law, Ethan, hadn't had time for a honeymoon after their quickie Las Vegas nuptials six months ago. Last month they'd flown to Australia, where it was still summer, for an extended road-trip honeymoon.

"She gets back to Nashville on Valentine's Day but won't return to work until the week after," Loretta answered.

Tammy nodded. "Thank…"

"Holy Moley!" Victor bellowed from the other side of the room.

Again, his outburst attracted the attention of the department heads seated at the table.

"For goodness' sake," Loretta said. "The entire room doesn't have to be privy to your circulation problems. I'm no spring chicken, but you don't hear me squawking about every little twinge."

"It's not me. It's…" Victor turned away from the window. He wore a stunned expression on his face. "Cole, I think you should take a look at this."

Concerned, Cole rushed to her stepfather's side. The older man pointed out the window, and Cole looked in the direction of his finger.

"What the…?" Cole blinked.

He stared dumbfounded at the electronic billboard in the distance, unable to believe what he was seeing. The gasps of the employees who had followed him to the window filled Cole's ears.

No, the hell she didn't.

The ad for Burger Tower's mouthwatering burger was gone. In its place was an advertisement for Stiletto Cosmetics, featuring the man in drag from the newspaper article photo. Even though it was a mile away, the ad flashed boldly against the gray winter sky.

The faux old lady wore the same lopsided gray wig, a hideous paisley dress and a thick coating of outdated makeup. He was juxtaposed against a chic young woman in skintight leather pants and high heels.

Cole's molars ground against each other as he glared at the caption—Stiletto: Not Your Granny's Makeup. It was scrawled across the bottom of the ad, in the same shade of red as Sage's lipstick, as if she'd signed it personally.

The blasted woman knew he'd see it. He'd told her he could see this billboard from his office window.

He felt a nudge at his side, and Loretta handed him a pair of binoculars she'd somehow located in the minutes since everyone had gathered at the window. Her efficiency still amazed him. No wonder his mother, Victor and now Cole gave her insolence a pass.

Peering through the binoculars, Cole zeroed in on the billboard. Magnification only made the damn thing worse.

"Looks like you poked the wrong bear." Loretta's gravelly words went into his right ear.

"Stiletto's owner is not just good-looking, she's ballsy,

too." Victor snorted in his left ear as Cole stood between them, binoculars still trained on the offensive sign in the distance.

Bring it!

Sage's taunt and his own rising anger drowned out the voices of his secretary and stepfather. Anger mingled with the respect Cole grudgingly had to give her. This was something he would have done, if his attraction to her hadn't thrown him for a loop.

He continued to stare at the heavily made-up man on the billboard, silently ridiculing Espresso. The insult was just the kick in the behind he needed to make his next move.

"This meeting is adjourned," Cole said firmly as he turned away from the window.

His department heads started to file out of the room, still buzzing about the billboard. Cole glanced at Loretta, who was looking at Stiletto's website on her tablet computer. News of the Valentine's Day event dominated the page.

He smiled to himself and called out to two of the retreating department heads. "Tate, Barnes, I'll meet you both in my office in five minutes," he said. "You too, Vic."

"What are you up to?" Loretta asked.

"I'll fill you in when we get to my office," Cole said.

It was time he showed the bear the consequences of taunting a tiger.

Chapter 6

Sage slowed her run to a walk as the small, modest house came into view.

She had repaired the sagging porch, patched the roof and painted the faded exterior paint, and there was still more renovation to be done. But the wreath made of painted pinecones and blue grosgrain ribbons hanging on the front door gave her home a certain charm.

The sight of the tiny house never failed to make her smile. Only fifteen years of mortgage payments remained before it was all hers. Once she paid it off, she'd never have to worry about being displaced or shuffled between homes again.

Sage swiped at the sweat dripping down her face as she walked up and down the length of her driveway to cool down. The early-morning three-mile run was the price she paid for her junk food habit.

She yanked the iPod earbuds from her ears, and the

sound of her sneakers crunching against the driveway's crumbling asphalt replaced the thumping beat of her workout playlist. Repaving the drive was another one of the items on the endless to-do list she'd amassed since becoming a homeowner last year.

She'd get to them all eventually. Right now her focus was on getting the house's interior up to par and building up the one thing she owned outright—her company.

Sage grinned. The thought of Stiletto brought to mind the new electronic billboard ad that had starting running yesterday. No doubt Cole Sinclair had seen it by now. Her grin morphed into a snicker as she imagined his reaction.

Damn, she wished she could have been the proverbial fly on the wall.

She stopped midstep as a second thought occurred to her. She'd better be on the lookout. The man would be out to get even. Sage was sure of it. In his shoes, she'd certainly be eager for some payback.

"Boo!"

Startled, Sage nearly jumped out of her sneakers.

A giggle sounded from the hedge she'd planted to replace the dilapidated picket fence separating her and her neighbor's properties.

Sage sighed and shook her head. So much for being on her guard. "I heard you laughing, so you might as well show yourself," she called out.

The bushes rustled, and a kid dressed in a fleece robe that covered superhero pajamas emerged. "Did I scare you?"

"Of course not," Sage said. "You hide in the bushes and shout boo at me every morning. No shock factor."

The kindergartener's hopeful face drooped, but a moment later his eyes narrowed with suspicion. "Then why'd you jump?"

"I didn't jump," Sage fibbed. If the little monster knew he'd actually gotten her this time, there would be no stopping him.

"Yes, you did. I saw you." He flashed her a triumphant snaggletoothed grin. "Got any Skittles?"

Sage reached for the zipper on the pocket of her jacket to pull out the packet of candy she put there every morning before she set out on her run.

"Kenny!" A voice bellowed over the hedge. "Kenny Hinton if you sneaked away from the breakfast table to pester our neighbor again, you're going to be in big trouble, Mister. Big trouble."

The front door of the house next door slammed.

"Uh-oh." The boy looked over his shoulder and then back at Sage.

Yanking the candy from her pocket, she tossed it to him. Kenny caught it and quickly hid it behind his back.

"I'm not bothering her, promise," the boy said moments later.

Evie Hinton peered over the hedge at her wayward son, two mugs of coffee in her hand. "March yourself right back into the house and finish your cereal. Don't get up from the table until you've eaten every bite."

The petite redhead passed one of the steaming mugs over the shrubbery to Sage as they both watched the little boy trudge back into his own yard and into the house. "Jeez, it's like living the movie *Groundhog Day*. Same thing every morning," Evie said.

"He's not bothering me." Sage wrapped both hands around the mug to warm them.

"You say that every morning, too."

It was true. She didn't consider herself much of a kid person, but Kenny had been the first person to welcome her to the neighborhood. Both he and his morning visits had grown on Sage. They made the child in her who had been shuffled between homes feel at home.

"And the two of you aren't fooling anyone, you know." Evie sipped her coffee. "I'm going to send you the dental bills when all that candy you slip him rots his teeth."

"What teeth? He's barely got any."

Evie laughed. "You got me there. Seems like the tooth fairy stops by our house every week."

Sage took a sip of coffee. She closed her eyes, briefly absorbing its warmth and caffeine. The notes of chocolate and coconut in her neighbor's coffee beans made everyday mornings feel like an occasion.

"Oh, do you think you'll be able to help me out with his birthday party in a few weeks?" Evie asked. "Kenneth will be on the road, and when it comes to kids' parties, most of the other parents tend to dump and run."

"Dump and run?" Sage wasn't familiar with the term.

"Dump their brats off and run like hell."

Sage laughed and readily agreed to help supervise the pizza party. Evie was always doing things for her, and she rarely got an opportunity to reciprocate.

"Kenneth due back tonight?" Evie's truck driver husband had been hauling a load of appliances to Miami.

The redhead shook her head. "Tomorrow," she said. "I'll be busy with your order tonight."

Sage had discovered she lived next door to a crafter extraordinaire shortly after moving in. Evie had stopped by to welcome her to the neighborhood, bearing a handmade door wreath fashioned from twigs, burlap and artificial sunflowers.

The wreath was stunning, as were the others the stay-at-home mom fashioned and hung on both their doors every month.

Evie had insisted her craft projects were just a hobby.

However, as the idea for Stiletto's first-ever event began to take shape, Sage knew she wanted her neighbor to make the centerpieces that would adorn the tables at the Valentine's Day morning affair.

"Keep in mind, I'm not complaining. Certainly not about the check," Evie said. "I'm still thrilled you even asked me."

It had been a good decision, Sage thought. Her neighbor had suggested adding a chocolate candy buffet, so in addition to making the centerpieces, Evie was also hand-crafting chocolates shaped like lipsticks, compacts and stiletto pumps.

"I'm the one who's thrilled. Our guests will be, too, when they see those centerpieces and gorge themselves on your chocolates." Sage drained the last of her coffee and stared almost mournfully into the bottom of her mug.

"Why don't you come inside for a refill?" Evie asked. "I've got a batch of cooling chocolates earmarked for Stiletto. They'll be ready to sample soon."

Sage was tempted and not just by the offer of more coffee and chocolate. It was still early, and she enjoyed chatting with Evie. They'd become friends over the months, and the Hinton home was one of the few places she allowed herself to relax. She opened her mouth to accept the invitation, but then remembered the salvo she'd fired at Cole Sinclair.

Kenny wasn't the only one who'd be lying in wait for her. She'd have to keep her guard up for the foreseeable future.

"Not today." Sage handed the empty mug back to her neighbor. "I'm going in to work early. I want to make extra sure everything goes smoothly."

Evie smiled over her mug. "That's probably a good idea." Her eyes brightened. "I saw the billboard."

Sage had told her friend what she was planning a few mornings ago. Unlike Amelia, Evie didn't try to warn her off teaching the big, bad millionaire a lesson. Instead, she'd practically doubled over laughing and wished her luck.

"I didn't know you drove all the way downtown to look at it," Sage said. "Well, what did you think?"

Evie shook her head. "I thought it was even more hilarious than the mock-up of the ad you showed me the other morning, but I didn't go downtown. It was on the news."

"The news?"

"Yeah, I was watching the story on it until Kenny caught my back turned and escaped the breakfast table." Evie tapped one of the now-empty mugs against her forehead. "Oh, no," she groaned. "Tell me I didn't send my kindergartener into a kitchen filled with cooling candy?"

Sage winced. "You did."

"Kenny!" Evie shouted as she sprinted through her yard toward her house.

A small figure came to the Hinton's door in response, and Sage could see from her driveway that his face was covered in chocolate.

"Oh, Kenny." Evie said.

Sage turned to her own house, leaving her exasperated friend to her charge. It was time for her to get dressed and get to work. She had her own baby to keep a watchful eye on while trying to anticipate Cole Sinclair's next move.

An hour later, Sage sat at her desk reviewing the list of RSVPs from social media beauty influencers across the country.

It was a task Amelia had assigned to another member of the Stiletto staff and personally overseen, but this billboard thing had Sage jumpy. She continued to scroll through the names, excited to see it read like a who's who of beauty bloggers and YouTube makeup gurus—all with huge followings.

The phone rang, and Sage jerked so hard she nearly fell off her office chair. She'd gone from jumpy to downright paranoid.

"For goodness' sake, Cole Sinclair isn't the boogeyman," she muttered aloud. "The only person waiting to ambush you is Kenny." And she wouldn't let the kid get the drop on her again.

The office phone stopped ringing, but immediately started up again. Sage was the only one there. With the exception of the security guard stationed in the foyer of the factory-turned-office-building, she was probably the only person around. It would be at least a half hour before Stiletto's staff and the workers for the various other businesses filed into work.

Sage debated letting it go to voice mail so Amelia could deal with whoever it was later. However, she saw the word *international* flash across the caller ID screen and curiosity drove her to answer.

A heavily-accented male voice greeted her. *"Buon giorno. Sage Matthews, per favore."*

"You're speaking to her."

"Hold for Signora Bertelli."

Her grip on the phone tightened. *Bertelli?* As in the Italian designer?

Slow down. Sage snorted. As if Signora Bertelli would ever call her. It was either wishful thinking on her part or some kind of prank.

Any doubts about the caller's identity were cleared up the moment a woman's voice came over the line. Sage recognized it instantly from a documentary feature film on the designer she'd watched dozens of times on DVD.

"Ms. Matthews, this is Marie Bertelli," she said. The

clipped tones of Boston's North End permeated her words as she apologized for the early hour. "I told my assistant to try anyway. Like most successful businesswomen, I suspected your workday began early."

Sage's hand began to tremble, and she clutched the phone with both hands. She'd never been starstruck or intimidated by anyone. Her motto being that everyone, including celebrities, put their underwear on the same way—one leg at a time.

Yet, she couldn't help the feeling of total awe that washed over her at receiving a call from someone whose work, especially her business acumen, she'd admired for years.

"What can I do for you, Ms. Bertelli?" Sage asked. Despite her excitement, her voice never lost its carefully honed cool.

"I read an article about you and your company in the international edition of *America Today* a few weeks ago," she said. "I was intrigued, so I asked my sisters to bring me a selection of your lipsticks when they came to visit."

An Italian-American born and raised in Boston, Bertelli had earned her undergraduate degree in fashion design from the Fashion Institute of Technology and an MBA from the prestigious Wharton School of the University of Pennsylvania.

The oldest daughter of an African-American mother and Italian father, she had relocated to Milan to work for the fashion house founded by her paternal grandparents.

"I loved the lipsticks," Bertelli said. "Especially the deep vampy purple one. I've had it on all day and received nothing but compliments. Darn it. I left the tube in my purse, and the name escapes me."

"One-Night Stand." Sage supplied and made a mental

note to have Amelia ship an entire case of the shade to her first thing this morning.

"Well, Ms. Matthews, it's definitely made a Stiletto fan out of me," she said. "Speaking of which, I had another reason for contacting you. I want to personally extend an invitation to you to attend the Bertelli runway show this month during Fashion Week here in Milan."

Sage froze as the invitation sunk in and then pressed her lips together to keep from screaming an excited yes in the woman's ear. She exhaled slowly in an effort to quell her excitement.

"Thank you, but I'll have to check my February calendar," Sage began, knowing full well she'd do whatever was necessary to make this trip happen.

"Of course," Bertelli said. "My secretary will be in touch. I really hope you can attend."

The two women spent a few moments exchanging pleasantries before ending the call. Sage was returning the cordless phone to its base when she heard the front door to Stiletto's main entrance open.

"Amelia," she called out from her desk, knowing the young woman was always the first of her employees to arrive. Her assistant would be ecstatic when she heard.

Sage opened her mouth to call out again just as the last person she expected to see filled the doorway of her office. *Cole Sinclair.*

She blinked, her mouth still hanging open, and then Sage snapped it shut before she started to drool. He looked different today. His expensive designer suit was replaced with casual attire, the effect coaxing her long-dormant hormones out of retirement.

Sage ignored how his height left scant inches between the top of his head and the door frame, and the way his jeans hugged the muscles of his lean thighs. Then she convinced herself his sweater, which appeared to be milled from the softest cashmere, didn't tempt her to make a pillow out of his broad chest.

Cole wore a leather bomber jacket in a shade of deep olive that was more stylish than the classic black, yet didn't detract from its bad-boy appeal.

Sage licked her suddenly dry lips. He looked good.

"No. It's not Amelia," he said, the melodic baritone threatening to lure her into a trance. An almost imperceptible spark flared in his dark-eyed gaze. It said without words that the blasted man knew she'd been admiring the view.

Straightening in her chair, Sage fixed her face with her most intimidating glare. "What are you doing here?"

"Good morning to you, too." He rested a shoulder against the doorjamb, and for the first time she noticed he hadn't come empty-handed. He held a green-and-white box in one hand. Its aroma wafted from the doorway, smelling as good as he looked.

"How'd you get past the security guard?" The question was nearly drowned out by the racket coming from her rumbling stomach. Sage narrowed her eyes. "You bribe him?"

A hint of a smile lifted the corners of mouth as he nodded. "It cost me two Krispy Kreme doughnuts." He inclined his head toward the box. "The rest are for you."

"But you of all people should know I can't be bought."

His smile deepened, revealing a dimple she hadn't seen before. "They're hot."

Me, too, thanks to you. Sage crossed her legs under her desk. She intended to keep them that way until this surprise visit of his was over.

"Are you sure I can't tempt you?"

Her stomach growled again as the smell of doughnuts

filled the office. Sage huffed out a sigh and gave into it. "Well, since you're already here."

He pulled away from the door frame and strode toward her with the ease of a man comfortable in his own skin. Bringing his free hand from behind his back, he produced a bouquet of brilliant yellow flowers.

"Also for you."

Sage eyed his offering. The cheerful mix of sunflowers, yellow Gerber daisies and alstroemeria blooms instantly brightened her office. They'd be a sweet gesture coming from anyone else. However, Cole Sinclair had an agenda. One that conflicted directly with hers, and she'd best not forget it.

Finally, she rose from her chair and took the flowers from her nemesis's outstretched hand. She hesitated before bringing them to her nose to inhale their sweet scent. "These aren't laced with hemlock, are they, Mr. Sinclair?"

"It's Cole, remember?"

"Well, Cole." Sage continued to inspect the sunny bouquet. "Did you hide a listening device in these posies that would make you privy to my office secrets?"

He chuckled. The deep, rich rumble made her toes curl inside her five-inch heels. One brow lifted as his brown eyes bored into hers. "Have you done something that would make you feel paranoid around me?"

"I take it you've seen the billboard." Sage acknowledged the obvious.

He nodded. "Oh, I saw it all right."

Rounding her desk, she crossed the room and stepped out into her outer office. She retrieved paper plates and a vase from a cabinet. When she returned, Cole was lifting the lid on the box of doughnuts, which he'd deposited on her desk. Sage passed him the paper plates and stuffed the flowers into the vase. Cole topped one of the paper plates with a warm glazed doughnut and handed it to her, along with a napkin imprinted with the doughnut chain's logo.

"I brought you coffee, too, but your security guard appropriated it as part of the bribe," he said.

"Would you like some?" Sage told herself it was the least she could do since he'd come bearing gifts. "It'll only take a second. My assistant insisted on one of those fancy single-serving brewers for our offices."

"No, thanks. I'm an earlier riser. I've already had coffee this morning, plus I ran three miles."

Sage told herself it wasn't another one of the similarities they shared. Plenty of people ran three miles and drank coffee in the morning.

He plucked a glazed doughnut from the box. "But I'll take one of these off your hands."

Leaning shoulder-to-shoulder against the front of her desk, they chewed simultaneously as they each polished off a doughnut. Sage broke the brief silence. "While I'm not entirely shocked to hear from you today, this isn't at all what I expected."

"Let me guess, you were waiting for me to call or storm in here ranting, ready to take your head off."

"Something like that."

He helped himself to another doughnut and placed a second one on her plate. "I'd be lying if I said it wasn't my visceral reaction. I was furious."

"I'll bet," Sage said. "But you seem pretty chill now." *Suspiciously so*, she thought.

"You can't think when you're angry." Cole bit into his doughnut and slowly chewed.

"And I take it you've been thinking."

"Oh, yeah." He sounded casual and friendly, but there was no mistaking the unspoken promise in his seemingly innocuous words. Sage heard it loud and clear: *watch your back*.

"So is this all part of your strategy?" She glanced over her shoulder at the flowers and half-empty box of doughnuts on her desk.

"Actually, the flowers are my way of acknowledging that the billboard was a brilliant move on your part. I foolishly underestimated you," he said, "and you found a way to make me pay for it and at the same time advertise your brand."

Sage scanned his face, unable to believe what she was hearing. This time he'd genuinely shocked her, and she had to do a double take.

Not many men, or people for that matter, were able to openly admit to a mistake or being bested. Yet Cole had done so with no reservations. Once again, he'd raised himself in her esteem.

Too bad he was after her company.

"Bravo." Cole inclined his head in a slight nod. "In your shoes, I might have done the same thing. After all, the best defense is a good offense."

Sage blinked. Those had been her exact thoughts when she'd hatched the idea for the billboard. It was becoming increasingly harder to brush off their similarities as mere coincidences.

"I don't suppose this makes us even," she said finally. Deciding to stop at one doughnut, she placed the plate bearing the uneaten one on her desk.

Having already demolished his second pastry, Cole wiped his hands with a napkin and tossed it in the wastebasket. "Not by a long shot."

He turned and focused his attention on her, leaning in until his face was scant inches from hers. "Besides, you have something I want." Sage shivered as the deep voice dropped to a husky whisper. His warm, sweet breath fanned across her face. "Now I want it even more."

Sage slammed her eyes shut and swallowed hard, silently willing the parts of her body shifting into Overdrive back to into Neutral. She should have stayed behind her desk with her legs tightly crossed, because this man was on the verge of talking the panties right off her.

When she opened her eyes, his gaze was locked on her lips.

"Is this your idea of keeping friends close and enemies closer?" The mocking tone she'd hoped for fell flat, her question echoed in her ears like a breathless pant.

"You're not my enemy, Sage," Cole murmured. "You're a challenge." He raised his hand and brushed his knuckles down the side of her cheek. "And I do love a challenge."

Clearheaded, a snappy comeback would have been on the tip of Sage's tongue. However, her brain had taken the backseat in her headspace, allowing a wave of longing so powerful it drew her to him like he was magnetized, to take the wheel.

"That lip shade is beautiful on you." His eyes never leaving her lips, Cole swiped the pad of his thumb across a sticky spot near the corner of her mouth. Sage stood mesmerized as he slowly licked the sugary glaze from his thumb, while her imagination conjured up illicit images of him licking her *everywhere*.

"What's it called?" He asked.

"Taste Me."

"You just read my mind." Cupping her chin in his hand, Cole leaned in and his brushed his lips against hers.

Sage steeled herself against the pleasure of the brief contact. The protective wall guarding her emotions cautioned her to put an end to this, before she lost control. She lifted her hands to his chest with every intention of pushing him away.

Before she could, Cole withdrew and stared into her

eyes. "Kiss me, Sage," he said, the deep melodic tone both a plea and a demand. "And *bring it*. Don't hold back."

Sage shivered at the sexy command. She was a woman accustomed to giving orders, but right now she wanted to follow his…just this once.

Fisting the sweater in her hands, she tugged him to her and kissed him hard. Sage felt his arm around her waist as he pulled her flush against him.

She gasped and Cole deepened the kiss. His tongue swept inside her mouth and slowly stroked hers. He tasted of doughnuts, sinfully sweet, and if her body's reaction to him was any indication, the man was just as addictive.

Encircling her arms around his neck, Sage melted into his hard body. She savored the languid movements of his mouth that were somehow reminiscent of the cadence of his easy Southern drawl. Absorbed in the sensual demands of his tongue and the bulge pressing against her belly, she lost track of time and place.

Cole wrapped his free arm around her. His hand gripped her ass, and she moaned as he ground against her. It was all too much, and at the same time, not enough.

"Morning! What are you doing here so…"

Sage jumped at the sound of the all-too-familiar voice. Cocooned in Cole's powerful embrace, she turned to find Amelia standing in her office doorway, mouth wide open.

Damn, Sage thought at the exact same moment Cole muttered the expletive aloud. She extricated herself from his arms and watched as he ran a hand over his short-cropped hair. The expression on his face mirrored her thoughts. A few moments more, and they would have both been naked, tasting more than each other's mouths.

Sage exhaled. By now her assistant had recovered enough for her initial surprise to have morphed into a grin too wide for her face.

"Cole Sinclair, this is my assistant, Amelia Brown," Sage said, regaining her composure.

Amelia looked pointedly from Cole and back to her, still grinning like a loon.

Sage shot her a glare, and the young woman quickly excused herself. "Carry on, General," she said, as she exited. "I'll be at my desk if you need me, reading one of my *far-fetched* romance novels."

Chapter 7

Cole grasped Sage's hand, wishing the contact would whisk them back to the moment before her assistant had interrupted. When her body heat had seeped through his clothes, and he could taste her sweet surrender as she sighed into his mouth.

"I appreciate both breakfast and the company," Sage said matter-of-factly.

He raised a brow to indicate her casual tone wasn't fooling him. Not after the kiss they'd just shared.

She met his gaze head-on. "Anything more would be a bad idea."

"Why? We're both adults, and neither of us has felt this attracted to anyone in a very long time." He ran his thumb along the back of her hand. It trembled in his before she pulled away. "Don't bother denying it," he continued. "You want me just as much as I want you."

"We both know it's more complicated than that."

"It doesn't have to be," Cole countered.

Sage shook her head slowly, defeating any hopes he had of picking up where they'd left off. "You want more than I'm willing to give."

"Are we talking about your company *or you*?"

"Both."

She rounded her desk, and he turned to watch her slide into the chair behind it. Taking the hint, he prepared to go.

"You're making a mistake," he said. "On both counts."

The cold morning air greeted him as he walked back to his black Dodge Challenger. Too bad it wasn't a kick in the behind, Cole thought.

What was the matter with him?

The same man who'd shown no mercy when going after companies to add to the Force Cosmetics portfolio turned into an amnesiac in this woman's presence.

One look at that pink-painted frown on her angelic face, and he'd promptly forgotten his reason for showing up at her office. A glimpse of her legs in those heels and pencil skirt, and Cole had barely recalled his own name.

He started up the car, and briefly debated whether to return to his town house on the other side of town to change or wear one of the suits he kept at work. Sage Matthews still had his mind, making the simplest of decisions difficult.

Her throaty whisper echoed in his head as he automatically drove in the direction of the Espresso building.

Taste Me.

Cole had come within seconds of clearing her desk with a single swipe of his arm, shoving that skintight skirt up to her waist and tasting her until his name fell from those pink-slicked lips over and over again.

Cole licked his own lips at thought.

"Shake it off, man."

He merged the muscle car onto the expressway. Good

thing his next move to convince Sage to sell him Stiletto was already in place, and like her in-your-face tactic, he'd designed it to do double duty.

Cole waited for the smug sense of satisfaction he'd gotten every time he'd thought about what he had in store. The feeling eluded him. That damned kiss remained on his mind along with the quick glimpse of vulnerability he'd seen in her eyes.

He shifted lanes as the downtown skyline came into view, speculating on whether to follow through with his plan. He'd never let the personal creep into business before.

You've never encountered a woman like her, either.

He was still debating if he should call it off when he exited the expressway. The morning rush hour had yet to start, and the streets leading to Espresso's headquarters were clear.

A traffic light switched from yellow to red, and Cole braked. Perhaps he should try a more low-key tactic to convince Sage to sell Stiletto. Maybe...

Then he caught it out of the corner of his eye—that blasted billboard. He studied the insult to his family business, which could be seen for miles. It hadn't changed since yesterday. The same man in drag stared back at him mocking his mother's life's work.

Fortunately, the flashing reminder made Cole's goal crystal clear. Time he started thinking with the head on his shoulders instead of the one below his waist. He'd show Sage Matthews the lengths he'd go to in order to get his hands on Stiletto.

In the long run, it was the best thing for him, Sage and their companies.

Seconds later, the light turned green, and Cole made a left and parked in the garage across the street from the Espresso building. His mobile phone rang as he crossed the street. Retrieving it from his jacket pocket, he saw the international caller on the small screen.

Cole answered and a woman's voice came through the line.

"*Ciao*, Cole. It's Marie Bertelli."

Marie? This was a surprise. He hadn't talked to her in years. Not since he was still with Force Cosmetics, working out of their European headquarters in Milan. He briefly wondered what she wanted, but figured he'd find out soon enough.

Automatically switching to Italian, Cole greeted her and inquired about her grandparents, who had always been gracious to him when he lived in Italy.

Marie stopped him. "Oh, Cole." She tut-tutted. "I speak Italian all day long. Talk to me in English, so I can hear my native tongue tinged with your exquisite Southern drawl."

"What can I do for you?" Her casual tone and pleasantries didn't fool him. Marie Bertelli wasn't one for idle chitchat. Neither was he.

Her soft sigh sounded through the phone as he nodded at the security guard, who held the door open for him. "A few weeks ago, I read the most interesting article about you in the international edition of *America Today*," she said.

Cole frowned. He didn't bother mentioning the article wasn't actually about him. Stiletto had been the subject of the story, while the cheap shot at Espresso had only been a paragraph and, of course, that damned photo. Similar to the one Sage had used for Stiletto's billboard ad.

"As someone who also runs their family's business, I can appreciate how busy you are nowadays," Marie said.

Cole walked to the bank of elevators and frowned at the signs on the doors. Two of the three were out of order, *again*. With an old building, it was always something. He hoped they'd be repaired by the time the workday started, and that the working one remained operable.

He'd have to make some decisions concerning the Espresso building soon. Hopefully, one they could all live with, including Victor.

Marie said his name on the other end of the phone, and he returned his attention to the call.

"I wanted to personally invite you to the Bertelli runway show later this month during Milan's Fashion Week," she said. "A new designer is making his debut for our men's line, and I think some of his pieces would be a perfect addition to your wardrobe."

Cole pulled the phone away from his ear briefly and gave it the side eye. He stifled the grunt threatening to escape his mouth. "Now, Marie, you know as well as I do that men's fashion week was *last month*. Besides, I'm sure the status of my closet isn't the real reason you're calling," he paused to calculate the time difference, "at three in the afternoon on a workday."

"Well, now that you mention it…" She hedged.

Here it comes, Cole thought. Marie Bertelli had a talent for finding an angle and twisting it around to benefit her family's business. A company she probably loved more than her husband and children.

"As you know, Italy has had its share of economic troubles in recent years. That combined with the long recession in America has taken a toll on our entire industry and Bertelli's profits," she said. "I need important people in the audience at our next show to attract the cameras and generate interest. I was hoping you could help me out. Also, Lola is on the list of models in the show."

He started to tell her there was no way he could go to Italy but hesitated. Fashion Week wasn't until the week after Valentine's Day. On the plus side, he could check on the condo he still had in Milan and see his baby sister.

"I'll be there," he said finally.

"Great," she said. *"Arrivederci. A presto."*

Cole swiped a finger across the small screen and shoved the phone back into his pocket. He knew Marie liked to stir the pot and couldn't help speculating what kind of drama she was cooking up now. Regardless, a few days an ocean away would be good for him. He could forget all about kissing Sage Matthews, and then his only interest in her would be acquiring Stiletto.

If his next move hadn't already convinced her it was her best option.

The remainder of the morning was a bust.

Sage spent half of it trying to ignore smug, knowing looks from Amelia. The rest of the time, she sneaked peeks at the buttery-yellow blooms on her desk and relived her early-morning visit from Cole Sinclair.

Some general she made. One brush of his hand against her cheek and her common sense had made a hasty retreat. She'd transformed from a savvy businessperson to a woman whose only ambition was getting in his pants.

Sage sucked her teeth in disgust as she pulled her red Dodge Challenger into her driveway and shut off the muscle car's engine. By noon, she'd given up on getting anything done in her office and decided to spend the remainder of the day working from home.

She lifted the huge bouquet from the passenger's seat. It had been a distraction at the office, and she didn't want to waste another workday staring at it. Or thinking about how she'd practically thrown herself at Cole Sinclair.

"Wow! Somebody really likes you."

Sage looked next door to see Evie hanging a new handmade wreath on the front door to usher in the month of February. Shaped like a heart, it was fashioned from a fluttery mix of red, white and pink ribbons.

"I'll be over with the wreath I made for your door in a few minutes." Evie winked. "Then you can tell me why you're home so early and all about that beautiful bouquet you're holding."

Dang flowers. Sage rolled her eyes skyward. They were destined to be today's topic of conversation whether she liked it or not. "We can have lunch," she said, resigned to her fate. "I ordered a pizza on the way home. The delivery guy should be here soon."

"Sounds good to me. Only we'd better not let it slip to Kenny. Pizza and visiting you are two of his favorite things. I'll have the first-ever kindergarten dropout on my hands if he hears he missed out on both."

A half hour later, Sage sat at her kitchen table with her neighbor, remnants of the pepperoni pizza they'd demolished between them.

Evie picked up one of the chocolates she'd made for the chocolate buffet at Stiletto's upcoming event and passed one shaped like a high-heeled pump to Sage.

"Now that you can't stuff your mouth with pizza every time I ask a question about your early-morning visitor, how about an answer?" Evie bit into a white-chocolate compact.

"What? I already told you everything. He brought doughnuts. We kissed. He left. End of story," she said. "Oh, I picked up the bags I ordered for the blogger event, pink with black lettering. They're in the trunk of my car. Did you want to see them?"

"Later." Her friend looked pointedly at the flowers and back to her. Ignoring Sage's attempt to change the subject, she continued, "I still don't get how you went from teaching a man from one of the city's most prominent families a lesson to this morning's lip-lock."

Sage bit the spiked heel off the piece of chocolate. She'd left out the detail about how, if Amelia hadn't walked in when she had, they would have done more than kiss. *A lot more.* She popped the rest of the candy into her mouth.

"It's hard to explain. Everything got twisted around. I'd expected arrogance and outrage on his part. I'd prepared myself for confrontation. Instead he was real."

"Real?"

Sage reached for another chocolate, this one shaped like a lipstick. "Real charming, real honest and completely genuine," she said. "He even admitted he'd made a mistake in underestimating me."

"Whoa." Evie paused, holding the chocolate she'd been about to pop into her mouth in midair. She leaned forward in her chair. "Did I hear you right? A man who can admit to being wrong."

She nodded, but her neighbor looked skeptical.

"I've been married ten years and I can count on one finger the number of times Kenneth has admitted to a mistake," she said. "He won't even acknowledge making a wrong turn."

While her physical attraction to the man was undeniable, it was in that honest, genuine moment that she found Cole Sinclair most appealing, Sage thought. When he let his guard down and gave her a glimpse into the real man beneath the money and power.

"I guess this means you two are square now," Evie said. "No more worries about retribution."

Sage resisted the urge to reach for more candy. "I wouldn't say that. He made it clear that he wants Stiletto."

Her neighbor shrugged. "But it's not for sale. End of story."

Sage wished it were that simple. This morning, she'd done a more specific internet search of Cole's tenure with beauty behemoth Force Cosmetics. Not only had he acquired a half dozen smaller companies for them, he'd also helped turn them from moderately successful ventures into household names.

"He has a lot of friends in the industry. A few well-placed phone calls on his part could shut a lot of doors in my face, which would put me in the position of having to reconsider his offer." The thought made her anxious, and she automatically made a grab for more chocolate.

"But he obviously likes you." Evie looked at the flowers. "You also mentioned you two having a lot in common."

Actually, what she'd said was they were a lot alike.

"He wouldn't do that to you, would he?"

Sage shrugged. "He might."

She and Cole were indeed a lot alike, and in his shoes, Sage couldn't be sure of the lengths she'd go to in order to acquire something she really wanted.

"But I can't work scared. It's just not the way I operate," she said.

"So what are you going to do?"

"The same thing I've done since I started my company—work hard." Sage made the decision as she spoke. "Right now that means doing everything in my power to make sure Stiletto's upcoming Valentine's Day event is a huge success."

It also meant getting her reaction to Cole under control. That meant no more melting at the sound of his hypnotic baritone. No more falling into his powerful arms. And his addictive kisses were definitely off-limits.

Sage thought about her upcoming trip to Milan. Marie Bertelli's invitation had come up at the perfect time. It would give her the time and space she needed to get her head together and shut down the part of her she feared was falling for Cole Sinclair.

Chapter 8

Stupid Valentine's Day!

Snatching a bouquet of cellophane-wrapped roses from her customer service manager's arms, Sage shoved them back at the woman's boyfriend.

"Give her this on your time." She glanced pointedly at the Timex on her wrist. "Right now, she's on Stiletto's time."

Hustling the third uninvited boyfriend of the morning out the door, Sage rolled her eyes toward the pale pink tulle they'd attached to the ceiling earlier. It was like dealing with a bunch of love-struck teenagers.

The very day she needed her team to be at their best, their brains had simultaneously turned to mush. All anyone cared about was sending or receiving roses, chocolates and, of course, those idiotic glassy-eyed teddy bears.

Sage scanned the smallest ballroom of Nashville's premier downtown hotel. Shortly, it would host a hundred of the most influential women in the beauty blogosphere, all with huge makeup-junkie followings.

Everything had to be perfect.

She double-checked the checklist in her head. The champagne rested in silver ice buckets. The pink swag bags, brimming with Stiletto goodies, including a mini-collection exclusive for event attendees, were lined up on two massive tables. Evie was putting the finishing touches on the chocolate buffet.

Sage groaned at the sight of her advertising manager, Joe Archer, yapping on his cell phone, a big sloppy grin plastered on his face.

What had possessed her to schedule this event for the morning of Valentine's Day? she asked herself for what seemed like the millionth time. She blew out a heavy sigh.

Not bothering with preliminaries, Sage walked over to the advertising manager, snatched the phone from his hand and ended the call. "Hold the personal calls until *after* the event, lover boy," she said firmly.

"It wasn't a personal call," Joe said through clenched teeth. "You just hung up on Freddy Finch."

Sage lifted her hands in a questioning gesture. The name meant absolutely nothing to her.

"The guy who dressed up like the old lady for the newspaper and then we hired for our billboard ad." The frown on her employee's face deepened. "He was in the middle of thanking us, because the billboard has led to more people in the seats at his drag queen show."

Sage winced. "Oh."

"Yeah, 'oh.'" Joe held out his hand. "So may I please have my phone back?"

Sage placed the phone back in his palm, just as she felt a hand at her elbow. Amelia was at her side. The young woman's lips were pressed into a firm line.

"What's wrong?" Sage looked around.

"You."

Still holding on to her elbow, her assistant steered her toward the closed door at the entrance of the ballroom. Sage yanked her arm away.

"What's gotten into you, Amelia?"

"I'm doing an emergency intervention because you're driving everyone absolutely bonkers."

Sage bit her lip, but not wanting to let her assistant have it in front of the other employees, she shoved the double doors open and walked out of the ballroom. Amelia followed.

Her assistant raised her hands. "Before you blast me, I was just trying to get you out of there before you had a revolt on your hands."

Sage opened her mouth to tell the young woman she was being ridiculous, but Amelia then rested her hands on her arms.

"You pay me and the people in that ballroom generous salaries," her assistant continued. "Now stop micromanaging and let us do the jobs you hired us to do."

Sage's first impulse was to argue. Instead, she clamped her mouth shut and nodded once. The young woman was right. If the strained looks on her team's faces were any indication, Sage's close supervision wasn't being taken as the help she'd intended.

Besides, she'd worked for enough jerks before starting her own company. She didn't want to become one. It was time for her to back off.

Satisfied, Amelia's arms fell to her sides.

Sage exhaled and leaned against a wall outside the ballroom.

"You coming back in?" Amelia asked.

"I'm going to wait out here a while. Get my event jitters under control." Sage crossed her arms.

"I'll come back for you in a few minutes, so you can

give everything the once-over before we open the doors for our guests."

Sage nodded her agreement. After Amelia disappeared into the ballroom, she closed her eyes and pressed the back of her head against the wall.

"Relax, everything is going to turn out fine." She whispered the mantra aloud, and then took a few deep breaths.

When she opened them she could hear the faint din of hammers, drills and machinery coming from the direction of the hotel's Grand Ballroom. The racket had died down considerably since she and her team had come in to set up at dawn this morning. Sage had spoken to the hotel manager, who assured her the workers would be done before Stiletto's event started.

Pushing off the wall, Sage walked around the corner to the larger ballroom to investigate. Approximately triple the size of the smaller Petite Ballroom she'd rented for Stiletto, the hotel's premier ballroom took up over half this floor of the hotel. Orange construction cones sat at both entrances, and strips of yellow-and-black tape stretched across the closed doors.

As Sage looked at it, she couldn't help hoping Stiletto's next event would be bigger, better and held in the hotel's premiere ballroom.

First, she had to make sure today was a success.

Sage glanced at her watch, and then looked up to see a woman she recognized from her YouTube videos, standing at the escalators. She was talking to a hotel worker, who was pointing the way to Stiletto's venue.

It was almost showtime.

Sage exhaled. She'd make a quick pit stop to the ladies' room to check her makeup before returning to the Petite Ballroom. The construction racket in the Grand Ballroom seemed to have slowed to just the occasional hammer or drill, so she didn't have to worry about it drowning out Stiletto's party.

She lifted her hand to push open the bathroom door. The sound of her name coming from the other side of it stopped her.

"Y'all are out of line." It was Amelia. "Sage is a good boss."

Sage knew she should either make her presence known or walk away. Nothing good ever came from eavesdropping. However, hearing her assistant use her real name threw her.

"Well, she certainly isn't this morning. Did you see the way she treated my fiancé? He brought me a giant stuffed panda, and she wouldn't even let him in the ballroom to give it to me."

Sage heard her assistant's voice. "Come on, Shelia—this is a big day for Stiletto. How would you have gotten anything done with a four-foot stuffed bear in your arms?"

A third voice chimed in. It belonged to Stiletto's customer service manager. "Maybe if she had her own man, she wouldn't be hating so hard on those of us who do."

"How do you know she doesn't have someone special?" her assistant asked.

Sage's stomach did a free fall as she recalled the scene her assistant had walked in on when she'd practically glued her mouth to Cole's. She touched her fingertips to her lips at the memory.

While she trusted Amelia not to gossip, Sage silently prayed the young woman wouldn't inadvertently reveal what she'd seen trying to defend her.

"You're joking, right?" Shelia's laughter came through the door. "What man could handle the general's hard ass?"

"One who likes seeing her wear his balls as earrings,"

the customer service manager quipped before joining in the laughter.

If her eyes had been laser beams, Sage was sure they would have seared two perfectly round holes through the bathroom door by now. However, a small part of her couldn't help feeling stung by the kernel of truth in their words. Sage knew she could be both tough and intimidating, and if her track record in the romance department was any indication, most men couldn't handle it.

A brief flash of the kiss she had shared with Cole popped into her head. No doubt the man could handle anything she threw at him, including herself.

Sage heard Amelia clear her throat, propelling her to force the wayward images of Cole from her head.

"If Sage wasn't such a hard-ass and a perfectionist, Stiletto would have failed like most start-up businesses do in this tough economy," she said. "And Shelia, you'd still be using that master's degree in medieval literature to take breakfast orders at the Waffle House."

You tell her, Amelia, Sage thought. She decided against walking in on them. It would only make them uncomfortable when she needed them focused on today's event. Besides, she didn't hire the other women to be her best friends. They were there to do their jobs, and they both did them well.

After retouching her lipstick in another bathroom, Sage started to make her way back to the Petite Ballroom. She heard the clamor of women chatting excitedly as she rounded the corner and was delighted to see a throng of amateur makeup mavens waiting for the doors to open.

Sage spotting a waving arm and then saw Amelia pushing through the crowd. "I've been looking all over for you," she said. "We're ready for inspection, General. As soon as you give your seal of approval, we can open the doors."

Sage noted the irony as she walked through the ballroom, taking in even the smallest details. While the rest of her employees used her name to her face and sneakily called her General behind her back, Amelia did just the opposite. There was never any subterfuge with her assistant. She remained honest and loyal, and said what needed to be said, even when Sage didn't make it easy.

Elevating the young woman to basically her second in command at Stiletto had been one of her wisest decisions.

Sage picked up one of the attendee name tags to doublecheck that it included Twitter and Instagram handles. She placed it back on the table and contemplated another run through her checklist.

"Stop stressing," Amelia said. "You made sure everything is perfect. What could possibly go wrong?"

"You're right. Let's open the doors for our guests and enjoy some of our hard work.

Ten minutes later, Sage stood on the dais at the front of the room filled with women wild for makeup. Their energy fueled her excitement and boosted her confidence.

"Welcome to Stiletto's first annual blogger appreciation social." She spoke into the microphone.

Applause erupted in the ballroom, and she paused before continuing the short speech she'd prepared. Her assistant had been right.

This was Stiletto's moment, and absolutely nothing could go wrong.

Cole took mental inventory as he stood in the middle of the hotel's Grand Ballroom. It had taken two crews working around the clock to transform it. Now all that was left were a few finishing touches.

"Looks like we just might pull this off," he said.

Loretta grunted and looked down at her ever-present

tablet computer. "I don't see why I had to leave the office to come down here to supervise. Your aunt sent her best workers."

"People tend to work faster and better with you watching them," Cole said. "It's your gift."

Fortunately, his father's side of the family was in the construction business, and they were able to take on the last-minute job. Cole didn't remember his father, but he remained close to the Sinclairs. One short conference call with his aunt and cousins explaining the situation and what he needed, and they were eager to help.

"Speaking of gifts." Loretta lifted her arm and shook the shiny gold bracelet around her wrist. "Tia brought me this from Hawaii last year. With all the crap I put up with, I'm expecting an even better gift when you return from Milan."

Cole snorted. "When it comes to selecting a present for you, crap is exactly what I had in mind."

Loretta frowned, but his cousin approached them before she could respond.

"We're all done here, cuz." Riley Sinclair returned the screwdriver she'd been holding to the tool belt hanging from her waist. "Just wanted to make sure you were satisfied with everything before the boys and I took off."

Cole looked briefly at Loretta, who nodded her approval.

"We're good," he told his cousin.

He checked his watch. "Loretta, would you go upstairs to the hospitality suite to check on our guests? I don't want any snafus this morning"

"Yes, sir," she said dutifully.

Cole's eyes widened...then realization dawned. It appeared his cantankerous secretary might be on her best behavior until he returned from Milan, gift in hand.

"I appreciate y'all taking this on at the last minute," he said, returning his attention to his cousin.

Riley shrugged and pushed away a dreadlock that had escaped the ponytail holder. "No problem. We're family." She frowned. "Although I haven't seen much of my favorite cousin since you've been back in town."

Cole felt a twinge of guilt. Riley was indeed his favorite cousin, too. Her easy, one-of-the-guys demeanor had made her one of his best friends, as well.

Before he'd left Nashville, they used to meet after work at Jake's sports bar the first Friday of every month. They would eat dinner, have a beer and catch whatever game was on the television.

"Mom misses you. I do, too." Riley punched his arm.

Cole winced. He was no lightweight, but years of wielding power tools meant even a playful punch from his cousin packed a wallop.

"I didn't hurt you, did I?" Riley grinned. "Don't tell me you've gone soft from having your backside parked behind a desk all day?"

Cole rubbed his arm. "Nah, it just tickled, that's all."

His cousin's laughter filled his ears.

"I miss you all, too," he said. "I've just been up to my eyeballs trying to straighten out the mess at Espresso…" He stopped talking, hating the way his reasoning sounded like excuses.

"I'm under strict instructions from Mom not to leave here until I have your word you'll come to Sunday dinner," Riley said.

His aunt had issued him a standing invitation to the weekly dinner with the family, however he'd only managed to make it once in the months since he'd returned.

"I will, soon. Promise," Cole said.

"Nope." Riley shook her head. "That's not going to cut it. Mom said dinner will be served at six o'clock tomorrow evening, and she expects you to be at the table. No excuses."

Cole could tell by his cousin's tone that if he didn't show up to dinner tomorrow, his aunt would send her three daughters out like a posse to round him up.

"I'll be there." His family had made his request their top priority. It was time he reciprocated and made them a priority. Besides, seeing his cousin had reminded him just how much he truly had missed them.

Riley beamed up at him as if he'd given her a gift.

"We can talk about reinstating our standing monthly date for a beer at Jake's," he said. Then he remembered he'd been gone a long time. More than likely, Riley had a better way to spend a Friday night than watching sports with a cousin. "Unless your boyfriend has you on lock down."

Riley snorted. *"Boyfriend,"* she said incredulously. "Things haven't changed that much since you left. The men in this town still prefer their women to be like petite, delicate flower blossoms, which leaves a gal like me strictly in the buddy category."

"Their loss," Cole said.

His cousin shrugged, but he could see a flicker of sadness in her eyes.

"Now, if there isn't anything else you need, my men and I are going to take off," she said. "I promised them a late breakfast at the Pancake Pantry if we got this job done on time."

Cole reached for his wallet. "Since it's my job, I'll cover it."

"Don't worry, I've already added it to your bill." Riley stuck two fingers in her mouth and blew out an earsplitting whistle that commanded the attention of every workman in the room. "Let's get out of here and get some pancakes, fellas." She turned to Cole. "We'll be back to take everything apart this evening."

Loretta returned to the temporarily renovated ballroom

as Riley's crew gathered up their equipment and began filing out of it.

"Oh, good luck." Riley stopped at the door and looked over her shoulder. "Hopefully, when that Matthews woman discovers what you've been up to, she won't take *you* apart."

Cole glanced at Loretta, waiting for her to take advantage of the opportunity to deliver one of her smart-aleck zingers based on his cousin's warning. She didn't. However, he didn't miss that the older woman's lips were clamped together so hard the color had drained from them.

"After needling me all week, no wisecracks about there being hell to pay when Sage finds out?"

"Nope." Loretta shrugged. "When she comes storming through those doors, as I expect she will at some point this morning, I intend to grab some popcorn and enjoy the show."

Images of Sage bursting into the ballroom popped into Cole's head. Big Afro, a defiant pout on her pretty painted mouth and walking on impossibly high heels.

He'd told himself repeatedly that this was business, not personal, but the thought of seeing her again excited him— in a very personal way.

A trio of Espresso employees surrounded him, breaking into his reverie with a series of updates. Preston was telling him about the computer station, and another employee was rattling on about extra cases of blush and mascara.

Their voices faded into the background as his thoughts once again centered on the impending explosion when Sage found out.

A smile tugged at the corners of his mouth. Oh, she'd bring it all right, and he could hardly wait.

Chapter 9

Sage's apprehension diminished as she mingled with the room full of internet beauty mavens. It had been silly to think Cole was lurking in the darkness plotting payback for the billboard episode.

He'd come at her eventually, she thought. Fortunately, it didn't appear he'd do it today.

Sage grabbed a bottle of water and twisted off the cap. Talking nonstop to Stiletto's guests had left her throat parched. She looked around the small ballroom at the clusters of young women gabbing excitedly. They were gushing over the items in the exclusive resort makeup collection, included in their swag bags, many of which would probably be up for sale on eBay by tomorrow.

More importantly, photos were being snapped and fingers were typing away on mobile phones. Their fervor was spilling over into social media time lines under the hashtags #StilettoValentine and #IHeartStiletto, and the news was being spread like gossip by their fanatical followings.

Sage took a long swig from the bottle. So far, her company's first event appeared to be a success. She thought briefly of Cole and his proclamation that he'd do a better job running Stiletto.

Too bad he wasn't here now. He'd see exactly what she could accomplish.

Maybe you just want to see him again?

She tried to dismiss the notion, but images of the kiss they'd shared in her office flitted though her head. Images so vivid she could almost taste his sugar-tinged mouth, feel his large hands on her ass and the sizeable bulge in his pants pressed against her belly.

Sage took another gulp of the cold water to cool off. Maybe the employees she'd annoyed earlier were right and she did need to find herself a man, preferably one that wasn't after her company.

Or didn't make her lose control like Cole Sinclair.

A young woman wearing smoky eye shadow and a nude lip gloss walked up to her. "Ms. Matthews, I'm…"

"You're Liptastic," Sage said, grateful for the distraction. "I recognize you from your blog. I also follow you on Instagram."

The women's eyes widened. "Really?"

Sage nodded. "I adored the photo you posted of your holiday favorites that had a tube of Santa, I've Been Naughty positioned next to a red, high-heeled marabou feather slipper, mug of cocoa and a peppermint stick."

Liptastic nudged Sage's side with her elbow. "I won't even mention what my fiancé did with that peppermint stick after he saw me in that lipstick."

Sage's eyes widened. "Oh, my."

"The name of that lip shade explains it better than I ever

could." Liptastic giggled and then winked. "Let's just say I had a smile on my face for days."

Sage laughed along with her, wishing there was a way to press this moment between the pages of a scrapbook. Then she could revisit it after a long, frustrating workday and remind herself why she'd chosen this business.

As her mother used to say when Sage was a little girl, "A little bit of makeup can change a woman's life."

Moving through the crowd Sage chatted up a half dozen more beauty gurus including @MakeupandMojitos, who had amassed a fanatical following from simply uploading a daily photo of her lip print on a cocktail glass, @BudgetGlam, known for creating million-dollar looks with dollar-store cosmetics and @PrettyEverything, whose YouTube channel had over a million subscribers.

She made her way over to the chocolate buffet, where Evie was restocking the candy. She grabbed a piece of milk chocolate shaped like a lipstick tube.

"I hope you have some stashed away for us at home," Sage said.

"Nope." Evie smiled. "It looks like your guests love chocolate as much as they do cosmetics. They're going to clean me out."

Sage looked around the room. A feeling of unease crept over her, and she turned to her neighbor.

"Is it just me, or does the crowd seem to have thinned out?" Sage looked at her watch. "We only started thirty minutes ago, and the event doesn't end for another hour and a half."

Evie glanced up from the candy compacts she was arranging on a silver tray and surveyed their surroundings. "Looks the same to me."

"I dunno…" Sage looked toward the doors. Three women were walking out of them.

Her neighbor followed her gaze. "You're being paranoid," she said. "Maybe they're just visiting the ladies'
room."

Sage nodded. "You're probably right."

Still, she couldn't seem to shake the feeling something
wasn't quite right.

"Stop worrying about nothing," Evie said. "This event
is a smashing success. You're a success. This is your moment, hon. Try to enjoy it."

Sage nodded. She was just being silly. Then she glanced
at the door. Two more of her guests were leaving. Maybe
they had Valentine's Day dates, she speculated. However,
they'd scheduled the event for the morning to avoid potential conflicts with lunch and dinner dates.

She glanced back at the door and saw another woman
walk out of it. The chatter had also begun to shift. Hushed
whispers intermingled with the bubbly conversations.

No, Sage thought. She wasn't being paranoid or imagining it. The crowd had definitely thinned out since her
welcome speech.

Both her eyes and her gut told her something was
amiss—neither had ever let her down.

Making her way through the diminishing crowd, Sage
was at the door when she felt a tap on her shoulder. She
turned to see a petite pixie of a woman she recognized instantly from YouTube.

"I was beginning to think I wasn't going to get to meet
you today," she said. "I'm…"

"The Wicked Glam Mother," Sage finished.

"Oh, so you've heard of me." The woman's brown eyes
twinkled with mischief.

Who hadn't heard of her? Sage thought. Known for her
hilarious and brutally honest reviews of both prestige and
drugstore makeup brands, the Wicked Glam Mother was

an internet sensation. She'd uploaded over three hundred videos, many of which had gone viral.

"Well, what did you think of the colors in our exclusive resort collection?" Sage asked.

So far the woman's reviews of Stiletto products had been overwhelmingly positive, but makeup lovers could be fickle, and a brand was only as good as the last collection.

The woman flashed an impish grin. "Wouldn't you like to know," she said.

"Yes, I would." Sage said. "But I don't suppose you're going to tell me."

The popular vlogger wagged a finger as she shook her head. "You'll find out later this afternoon, along with the rest of the world, when I upload my video."

Sage didn't bother trying to cajole it out of her, like the woman had obviously hoped she would. It wasn't her style. Besides, she recognized the deep berry shade on the Wicked Glam Mother's mouth. It was a lipstick from the resort collection the Stiletto team had dubbed A Good Lay.

As their conversation continued, Sage surreptitiously glanced at the door. Four of their guests had left, followed by another two.

What in the world was going on?

Finally, she was able to break free from the YouTube guru to investigate. However, Amelia and Stiletto's director of social media stopped her before she got to the door.

"I think we have a problem," her assistant said.

No kidding. "What's wrong?" Sage asked.

"People are walking out, and we're not even halfway through the event. Meanwhile, there are two new hashtags overtaking ours on social media time lines." Amelia inclined her head toward the social media director. "Show Sage what you just showed me."

Exhaling, Sage took the tablet and scanned the time line.

The hashtags #EspressoTakeover and #EspressoCosmetics jumped out at her as she read.

Free Valentine's Day makeovers with celebrity makeup artists. #EspressoTakeover #EspressoCosmetics

Get your Valentine's Day pretty on with the artists who create makeup looks for Rihanna and Beyoncé—for FREE! #EspressoTakeover #EspressoCosmetics

Cole, Sage thought. But he wouldn't…

She continued to glare at the tablet's screen as more messages appeared on the time line. An image of Cole in her office came back to her. Not the one of them kissing that had dominated her days and nights, but the expression accompanying his reply to her question about them being even after the billboard ad.

Not by a long shot. His words echoed in her head.

Cole Sinclair definitely would, Sage thought. Anger began a slow simmer in her gut, eclipsing the dread she'd felt just moments ago.

It kicked up a notch when she spotted a cell phone snapshot Liptastic had posted to social media showing off the results of her makeover with one of the celebrity makeup artists using Espresso cosmetics. She'd just talked to the woman, Sage thought. So much for brand loyalty.

"I'm not sure where Espresso has set up, but it has to be near the hotel for them to steal our guests," Amelia said.

Realization dawned and Sage closed her eyes briefly. "I have a hunch where they may be set up." A strong hunch, she thought.

Her assistant at her side, Sage walked out of Stiletto's event. They followed two beauty bloggers down a corridor and around the corner in the direction of the larger ballroom.

The thumping beat of music vibrated the carpeted floor beneath their feet as the Grand Ballroom came into view. Sage immediately noticed the doors were wide-open, and a banner with the words *Espresso Cosmetics Pop-Up Shop* hung above them. Her eyes zeroed in on the sign that had replaced the orange construction cones she'd seen earlier. It boasted free Valentine's Day makeovers by a list of ten celebrity makeup artists flown in from New York and Los Angeles.

"Damn." Sage muttered the word through clenched teeth.

She should have checked this room the moment she'd seen the workmen, instead of assuming the hotel was doing renovations. How could she have been so stupid? She should have known something was up—and who was at the bottom of it.

Sage stalked through the doors. She glanced around the huge room, which had been transformed into a temporary studio. Rows of tables were covered with lighted mirrors and stocked high with makeup, *Espresso makeup*.

Lines had formed by each table as defecting beauty gurus waited to have their faces transformed by the same artists who worked on the world's most beautiful faces.

Sage continued to scan the room until she spotted Cole standing in the midst of it all. He appeared to be having a conversation, but stopped and turned in her direction as if he'd felt her gaze boring into his back.

Their gazes connected, and even at a distance, Sage could see his brow raise and the slight incline of his head. He had been waiting on her.

"Mutha..." Sage swore, but the pounding beat of the music and accompanying rapper cautioning someone not

to mess with his money drowned out the rest of the word, and the string of curses that followed it.

"General!" Amelia, who was within earshot, admonished her.

Sage took a step forward, already anticipating giving Cole an earful. Her assistant caught her by the arm.

"You're not going to confront him, are you?" she asked.

"You bet I am." Sage practically salivated as she mentally calculated the steps between her and that infuriating man."

"Are you sure that's a good idea?"

"Do you not see what's happening? He sabotaged our event."

"Well, you did provoke him," the young woman pointed out. "If we're being completely honest, you started it."

Sage rolled her eyes so hard they nearly bounced off the ceiling. "I—I did no such thing." Fury made her stammer the words.

Amelia shook her head. "I'd assumed when I walked in on the two of you a few weeks ago going at it like the characters in my favorite romance novel, *Corporate Temptation*, that you and Mr. Sinclair had worked out your differences," she said. "What did you do to mess it up?"

"Me?" Sage ground out the question.

"Let's be real here—you can be abrupt." Her assistant narrowed her eyes. "And something happened to make him go from bringing you flowers and breakfast to purposely upstaging our event."

"Just whose side are you on?" Sage fumed.

Amelia sighed. "All I'm trying to do is get you to calm down before you go storming over to Mr. Sinclair and make things worse."

Calm down? Sage bit her lip to keep from unleashing on

her a tirade of words meant only for the ears of Espresso Cosmetics' CEO.

You can't think when you're angry.

Cole's words came back, and Sage inhaled a deep breath. As she exhaled an idea for extracting a little payback of her own began to form. Sage turned to her assistant. "Repeat what you just said."

"I was trying to get you to calm down."

"No, before that," Sage said.

"Oh, I was reminding you that I'd said the billboard, using a man in drag as a backhanded insult at Espresso, was a bad idea from the very beginning. *But noooo.*"

"Amelia, you're a genius." Sage threw her arms around the young woman in an uncharacteristic hug.

"Uh-oh." Her assistant stiffened. "You're making me nervous here."

Releasing her, Sage grinned in response.

Amelia's eyes widened before her lips firmed into a disapproving frown. "You're sprouting horns out of your head again, and that never bodes well."

"Never mind my head. I need to talk to Joe Archer." Sage cast a look in Cole's direction. He stared back at her, a half smile on his smug, handsome face. She noted again that he appeared to be waiting for her to pounce.

Turning back to her assistant, Sage suppressed a grin of her own. "Let's get out of here."

As they walked out the door, she heard Amelia sigh and grumble something about all hell breaking loose.

Chapter 10

Disappointment mingled with disbelief, as Cole watched Sage leave the ballroom. The polar opposite of the elation he'd experienced the moment he'd realized she'd arrived in all of her red-minidress and stiletto-booted glory.

He'd told himself all morning it didn't matter, yet he had found himself taking furtive glances at the door. Watching. Waiting.

Damn.

Cole continued to stare at the door. He'd seen the outraged expression on Sage's heart-shaped face and felt the heat of her temper from across the room.

"So she didn't take the bait, eh?" Loretta sided up to him.

Unfortunately, no, he thought, shaking off unwarranted dismay. He'd bargained on Sage's reaction. Expected her to march straight to him and treat him to a closer look of those spectacular legs showcased by what had become his absolute favorite dress.

"Doesn't matter," Cole said aloud. "This isn't about Sage Matthews."

"Isn't it?" His secretary's dark eyes looked right through him.

Cole averted his gaze and shoved his hands in his pants pockets. "This is about showing the owner of Stiletto Cosmetics the power Espresso still wields, despite our current image problems," he said. "We can take her company to heights she can't reach on her own."

"If you say so." Loretta glanced down at her tablet computer.

"I do," Cole reiterated. "And contrary to popular belief, I'm *your* boss."

"Well, if you want my advice..."

"I don't." Cole cut off the older woman, knowing it wouldn't stop her from having her say.

"All I'm saying is I'd grow eyes in the back of my head if I were you. If the look on her face when she left here is any indication, that young lady isn't done with you."

His mind rewound to kissing Sage in her office, and the warmth of her taut body penetrating his clothes as she melted into to him. He recalled the brief glimpse of vulnerability he'd detected in the depths of her soft brown eyes, when she momentarily dropped her guard and her need to be in control.

Cole hoped Loretta was right, because he certainly wasn't done with Sage, *not yet*.

He switched focus to the here and now. Sage was gone. He'd seen the last of her for today.

Cole tapped the top of Loretta's tablet. "So what have you done to earn your salary today besides give me unsolicited advice?"

His secretary grunted and inclined her head toward the makeup artists, who were still busy creating new looks for the beauty gurus they'd lured from Stiletto. "Spent a good chunk of it catering to the demands of these prima donnas you imported from New York and LA."

"Come on, they can't be that bad."

Loretta frowned. "This one can't work without a green smoothie made with coconut milk. That one needs an aromatherapy candle to clear the air of bad vibes," she said. "I swear they almost had me reaching for a cigarette."

"Delegate their requests to someone else." Cole didn't want the older woman to relapse and slip back into smoking. "Those cigarettes have left your voice gravelly enough. Every time you open your mouth, I look around for Darth Vader."

"Humph. No need for that now. I got fed up when the last one told me to find him a bendy straw to sip his coffee through," Loretta said. "I told him to do the job we contracted him to do, or else."

He wrinkled his face in confusion. "Bendy straw?"

"So the coffee won't stain his teeth," Loretta explained.

Cole lingered in the ballroom for another half hour. The room remained abuzz with excited bloggers, every makeup artist was busy and the lines for free makeovers had grown. By the looks of it, he'd succeeded in turning Stiletto's Valentine's Day event into an Espresso Cosmetics party.

There was nothing here his employees couldn't handle. Besides, without the underlying anticipation of seeing Sage again today, there was no reason for him to stick around.

Cole considered swinging by Burger Tower for an early lunch and pulled out his phone to place a to-go order. The red battery light flashed up at him, and he shoved it in back into his pocket. He'd call from his car, once he connected it to the charger.

A shriek of laughter reverberated throughout the room.

Cole, along with everyone else, turned toward it, and then his mouth gaped open.

The guy in drag, from the newspaper article and Stiletto's billboard, paraded through the ballroom in full old-crone regalia. He wore a huge sandwich board over an outdated floral print dress that read Ditch Granny's Makeup!

Sage.

She wouldn't. Anger seeped into Cole's bloodstream as the man began to work the room as though he was the guest of honor. Oh, but she definitely had.

"Look, it's the Espresso Granny!" A blogger yelled out over the music.

More outbursts of laughter joined the chorus.

The Espresso Granny?

"Oh, hell no." Cole's hands clenched into fists at his sides.

Crossing the room in three long strides, he effortlessly lifted "granny" by the collar until *her* white orthopedic shoes dangled above the floor.

"H-hey! What's going on?" The goateed man cowered inside the oversize dress.

"Get. Out. Now." Cole growled.

"Stop picking on Granny." A blogger called out.

"Yeah, give the old girl a break. It's Valentine's Day," a second voice shouted, causing yet another round of raucous laughter to erupt throughout the ballroom.

Cole released the interloper's collar and watched him stagger to his feet.

The man held up his hands in surrender, a straw purse dangling from the crook of his hairy arm. "Look, I don't want any trouble." His lips, coated in chalky pink lipstick, trembled as spoke. "I'm just doing my job."

"What job?"

"The one I hired him to do." A familiar voice said from behind them.

Cole whirled around and came face-to-face with the woman he'd spent the better part of the morning pining for like a complete idiot.

"Cole Sinclair, meet Freddy Finch." A humorless chuckle fell from Sage's lips. "Better known to you as Espresso Granny."

Struggling to keep a lid on the fury in danger of consuming his entire body, Cole spoke slowly. "Do you realize the damage you've just done?"

"Kind of like you sabotaging my event with this little shindig?" Sage matched his hard glare.

"It's hardly the same thing," Cole said. "In five minutes, you've managed to cement in people's minds the very image I've been battling. Months of hard work down the drain."

"Miss me with the sob story." She swiped at an imaginary tear. "You were pretty good at dishing out the payback, how does it feel to be on the receiving end?"

Freddy cleared his throat. "Um, excuse me. Have you decided what you want me—"

"What are you still doing here?" Cole barked.

Freddy flinched and turned to leave, but Sage caught him by the arm.

"He has every right to stay," she countered. "Like the sign outside the door says, this event is open to the public."

Freddy glanced from Cole to Sage. A fine sheen of perspiration covered his forehead, sending the thick coating of makeup sliding down his face.

Cole shoved his hands back into his pockets to keep from doing something that would make the onlookers accuse him of elder abuse. He kept his voice low. "If I have to tell you again, my foot is going to do the talking when I put it dead in your..."

Freddy hightailed it out the door before he could finish his statement, and Cole pivoted back to Sage. "You've gone too far this time."

"Unlike Freddy, I don't scare easily."

Cole opened his mouth to argue, but he spied a television news reporter and cameraman entering the ballroom. He inclined his head toward them, and Sage followed his gaze.

"I'm not finished with you, but the last thing either of us wants to do is plaster fake smiles on our faces and answer questions right now."

She grunted. "Two things we can agree on."

"Let's continue this elsewhere."

They ducked out of the ballroom's side door but found the space outside it teeming with beauty gurus spilling over from both their events. Their conversation was bound to get ugly, and Cole was sure Sage didn't want to have it out in the open any more than he did. Besides, between all the chatter and loud music, he could barely hear himself think.

She walked a few feet ahead of him as they looked for somewhere they wouldn't be overheard. Cole caught the sweet sway of her ass in that minidress and the needle heels of her thigh-high boots as she walked.

Remembering the stunt this woman had just pulled, he tried to look away. However, his traitorous eyes stubbornly refused and continued to enjoy the view.

Get a grip, man, he silently admonished when the sight of her made him want to slide his hands along her toned thighs until they gripped her hips as he drove into her over and over again.

Cole blew out a breath and reached deep for willpower

he hadn't known he possessed. He forced himself to think of the faux crone who, thanks to the woman in front of him, would be associated with Espresso in the minds of some of the internet's most influential beauty gurus.

It did the trick and put an abrupt end to his unwanted hard-on. With the blood flowing back to the head on his shoulders, he could think clearly.

"In here." Cole yanked opened the door to one of the hotel's utility rooms around the corner from the ballroom.

Sage stopped, turned on her heels and followed him inside, closing the door behind them. She switched on the light, and he glanced around what turned out to be a linen closet. It was a tight space, but it would do for the serious conversation they needed to have—*now*. The tablecloths, sheets and towels stacked on the surrounding shelves would also muffle the inevitable yelling.

She crossed her arms as she lifted her chin to glare up at him. There was a mulish set to her jaw. Cole tried to process how Sage Matthews made red-hot fury look, well, *hot*.

Again, he forced himself to think of the newly dubbed Espresso Granny crashing his event and making a damn spectacle.

"Just what kind of game do you think you're playing?" he asked.

"Me?" Sage's outraged eyes continued to blaze into his.

"Yes, you! This was business, pure and simple. You and that Freddy character made it personal."

"Don't you dare try to put the blame on me. You took it there when you insinuated I didn't have the know-how to grow the company I started at my kitchen table." She raised her voice to match his as she pointed a finger at her chest. "*My* company, Mr. Sinclair, and you'd best believe it's going to stay that way."

"I wouldn't bet on…"

A loud thump sounded against the door. Cole stopped midsentence, and they both turned toward it.

"Are you sure the general's in there?" A muffled voice asked on the other side of the door.

"I saw her go in a few minutes ago," A woman replied.

"Why would she be in a utility closet?"

"I don't know. Probably looking for a broom to ride on." A couple of guffaws followed their so-called joke.

Cole looked at Sage, and they both turned back to the door.

"Make sure you jam it in there tight."

"What the...?" Sage lunged for the door and twisted the knob.

Cole heard smothered giggles over the music blasting from the Grand Ballroom as the covert conversation continued.

"That ought to hold her awhile," a third voice chimed in. "Now the rest of us can enjoy the remainder of Valentine's Day, General-free."

Sage raised her fist and pounded against the door. "If you know what's good for you, you'll open this door right now," she shouted, and then tried the doorknob again.

Nothing.

Cole watched her hit the door harder and then kick it. "Did you hear me?" She yelled. "Let me out!"

She glared over her shoulder at him. "I could use some help here," she said. "In case it's escaped your notice, we've been locked in here."

Cole folded his arms across his chest and leaned against the shelves behind him. "What exactly do you want me to do?"

"Break the door down." She kicked it and winced. "Or use a credit card to pop the lock like the burglars do on television."

"In case it's escaped *your* notice, that door is made of steel, and unfortunately, my undergrad major was in chemistry not breaking and entering."

Sage blinked. "Chemistry?"

"You, too?"

She nodded once. It shouldn't have surprised either of them. Every time they were together, another similarity came to light. He held her gaze a moment, before she diverted her eyes and returned her attention to the door.

"Help!" She pounded on it again. "Help! Open the door! Let us out of here!"

"You're wasting your time yelling," Cole said. "Sounds like someone cranked up the volume on the music. Nobody can hear. Call the front desk on your mobile. They'll send someone up to open the door."

Sage held up her hands up. "I left it in my purse—we'll have to use yours."

"Battery died. I'd planned to charge it in my car but got sidetracked by that dumb stunt you pulled back in the ballroom."

"Dumb stunt?" She harrumphed, folded her arms and leaned her back against the door. "You had no business in that ballroom or this hotel in the first place."

Cole tilted his head to one side. "Speaking of stunts, do you have any idea who locked us in here? I didn't recognize the voices," he said. "I also don't remember seeing any military personnel around here, and I certainly would have noticed someone with the rank of general."

A flush of pink tinged her light brown face. She looked down at the floor as she mumbled an answer to the question.

"Speak up, I couldn't make out what you said over the racket of the music."

"It's me, all right?" She exhaled. "Some of my employees call me General behind my back, and they're the culprits."

Cole snorted, shaking his head. "Which puts us right back to this entire mess of a morning being all your fault. I hope you're satisfied." He shrugged off his jacket and tossed it on top of a stack of clean towels. "Who knows when we'll get the hell out of here now, *General*?"

He watched her mouth open, close and open again like a beached fish gasping for air. Red overtook the flush of pink staining her cheeks. The fire of their tempers sucked the oxygen from the tiny space, making it feel even smaller.

"How dare you?" Her teeth were clenched as she ground out the words. "Today was supposed to be all about Stiletto. You're the one who made a mess of it."

Cole glowered across the small space at her. "So what did you expect me to do after that billboard? Roll over and play dead?" He was sure anger had left him just as red in the face. "You told me to bring it. All I did was honor your request."

A noise that sounded like a growl emitted from her, before she advanced on him, all high heels and big hair. Again, Cole couldn't help notice, even pissed off, that Sage Matthews was the sexiest woman he'd ever seen.

Sage jabbed a finger at his chest. "Y-you have got to be the most arrogant, the most infuriating, the most…arghh!"

Cole's instincts took control. Wrapping an arm around her waist, he hauled her against him. The lightning-quick move caught her off guard, and he felt a whoosh of breath leave her body.

Huge brown eyes stared up at him. They softened as he examined their depths. God, she was beautiful, he thought. Her caramel-slicked lips beckoned, and while there was a part of him still annoyed with her, the rest of him wanted her, badly.

"We're probably trapped in here for at least another hour or two." He brushed his knuckles down the side of her cheek with his free hand. "Not Stiletto. Not Espresso. Me and you. The last thing I want to do is fight with you. *What do you want?*"

She swallowed hard. Cole could see the rise and fall of her breasts beneath her dress, feel her nipples bead against his chest as her breath came out in soft pants. Sage's body told him what she wanted. He just needed her to say it.

"If you won't tell me what you want, maybe the answer lies in that pretty lipstick you're wearing." Still holding her close, Cole leaned in and kissed her softly on the lips. She moaned, and his cock hardened instantly. "What's it called?"

Her eyes sparkled, and she bit her bottom lip before answering. "Lick Me."

Chapter 11

"My pleasure."

Cole's deep voice rumbled through her, and Sage melted. The velvety timbre slipped past her defenses, and she dropped her guard.

"I'm going to lick you until you're hoarse from screaming my name."

His promise made her drop her panties.

They hit the floor, and Sage quickly stepped out of them, kicking the scrap of black satin aside.

There were a myriad of reasons why this was a bad idea, but at this moment, with this man, she didn't give a damn about any of them. Cole had awakened a long-dormant desire only he could satisfy.

"Again, I have two words for you, Mr. Sinclair." Sage raised a brow. *"Bring it."*

With a swipe of his arm, Cole cleared a top shelf of sheets, sending them tumbling to the floor. Sage rested her hands on his biceps as he placed his hands on either side of her waist. He lifted her above his head as if she were weightless and gently deposited on the empty shelf's ledge.

His chin level with her knees, he lifted his gaze. "Oh, I intend to bring it, all right," he said, echoing their first conversation. "I just hope you can handle it."

Sage's bare ass shivered against the cool steel shelf, but the rest of her body was on fire, her core already wet with anticipation. "*Ooh.* That's mighty big talk. Let's hope your tongue can back it up.

Cole stuck a finger inside the scooped-neck collar of her dress. He pulled her forward until her face hovered inches from his, and then closed the distance between their mouths. He kissed her long and deep. His tongue owned her mouth as it teased and tantalized hers in a carnal pre-view of the coming attraction.

Sage moaned and squeezed her legs together, on the brink of climaxing from a single kiss. There was nothing lacking in this man's tongue game. *Nothing at all.*

Threading his fingers through her hair, Cole fisted a handful of the kinky curls. His grip tightened, and he tugged her head back to end the kiss. The primitive action sent a shiver from her scalp down to the tips of toes, which curled inside her thigh-high boots.

"Not yet," he said, reading her body's signals as if they were his favorite bedtime story.

Minutes ago, she'd banged on the door desperate to escape. Now Sage didn't care if it ever opened. The music coming from the ballroom further secluded them. Its pulsing beat drowned out the outside word.

She watched Cole take a single step backward. He grasped her calf in one hand as his other hand and his gaze traveled down the length of her boot-encased leg to her ankle.

"Damn." He closed his eyes briefly as if he were struggling for control and then he stared up her. The lust she saw in his dark eyes matched her own. "Later, I want to see you wearing nothing but these boots and me on top of you, but for now…"

He draped her leg over his shoulder until it dangled down his broad back. The motion raised the hem of her short dress to the tops of her thighs, and Cole pressed a kiss to the inside of the one resting on his shoulder.

Sage's teeth sank into her bottom lip when he placed his free hand on her other knee and gently pushed it aside, splaying her open for his perusal. The appreciative expression on Cole's handsome face made the discomfort of her last Brazilian wax worth it.

She leaned back, and braced her hands behind her as he buried his face between her thighs.

Cole licked her once, drawing out the movement as if he had nothing but time.

Then he did it again.

Oh, my God. Sage's eyes slammed shut, and she pressed her lips together to keep the scream reverberating in her head silent. She felt him pull back and opened her eyes to find him staring up at her.

"Unbelievable," he said. "You taste even better than you look."

He put his tongue back to work alternating long, languid laps with quick flicks, overwhelming her clit with a deluge of sensations. Bringing her to the brink, then holding back as she squirmed and begged for more of the exquisite torture.

"Don't stop, Cole. God, please don't stop." Her frantic pleas filled the room as he continued, licking and sucking until Sage thought she'd lose her freaking mind.

The first spasm hit, and she nearly bucked off the shelf.

Cole's strong hands slipped beneath her. He gripped her ass and pulled her even closer.

Sage arched her body toward him, calling his name as she rode his tongue to a shuddering orgasm that left her sweating and shaking like a junkie.

And like an addict, she was already craving another fix.

Cole lifted her off the shelf, and Sage slid down the length of his body. He kissed her hard and deep, his talented mouth still tasting of her.

"Wow." It was the only word Sage could manage. Even then it sounded like a hoarse croak.

Cole held her close, and Sage didn't miss the smug satisfaction in his smile or the rock-hard cock in his pants. She slid her hand between them and palmed his erection.

She raised a brow as she gently squeezed. "Impressive."

Cole hissed out a breath as his cock pulsed against her hand. "If you're impressed now, just wait until I get inside you."

Sage took a step back and tugged at his belt. "As you probably already know, Mr. Sinclair, I expect you to…"

"Bring it." He smiled down at her as they both uttered, what had unintentionally become their favorite catchphrase, simultaneously.

"I just hope I can handle it." Sage fanned herself with one hand and unbuckled his belt the other. She was reaching for his zipper when they heard a noise at the door.

Before they could register what was going on, it opened. A woman wearing a hotel uniform stood in the doorway. Concern creased her features.

For the first time, Sage noticed the music had stopped. Not only had this man made her lose control, she'd lost track of time and place.

"Someone said they thought they heard a woman screaming in here. Then there was a chair wedged against the doorknob." The hotel worker turned to Sage. "Are you okay, miss?"

Sage averted her eyes, trying to remember just how much screaming she'd done. "Uh…"

"She's good," Cole said, still holding her close. "Damn good," he whispered against her ear.

The hotel employee glanced from her to Cole, then pointedly at Sage's discarded underwear on the floor. "Sorry to disturb you."

The woman shot Sage another look, this one filled with pure envy. "Lucky heiffa," she muttered, as she walked away.

Yet, with the door open and them free to return to the real world, Sage didn't feel fortunate. Deep down, she wasn't ready for their interlude to end. Not yet.

Exhaling, she prepared herself to make and hear the awkward excuses that came in the aftermath of an unexpected sexual encounter. She knew, in this case, it was probably for the best. In this room, they were lovers. Once they stepped out of it, they were back to being adversaries.

"This has been…but…" she began. Still in Cole's arms, her gaze drifted toward the open door.

He placed his forefinger to her lips, before she could finish, and then used the same finger to lift her chin. "I'll understand if you feel differently, but I have to confess that I'm not ready for the real world to intrude on us just yet," he said.

Sage looked into his dark eyes as words continued to tumble out of his mouth. Again, she found herself drawn to Cole's honesty, sincerity and a vulnerability she suspected he rarely revealed.

He also had the courage to say aloud exactly how she felt, but couldn't bring herself to express. Sage didn't miss the irony of it. The same woman who faced her fears and took risks regularly in business shrank away from both in her personal life, especially in matters of the heart.

"There'll be plenty of time to focus on our respective businesses," Cole said. "Spend the afternoon with me."

There wasn't anything she wanted to do more. However, her sensible side, the part of her that wasn't light-headed from his kisses and still pulsing from the aftershocks of his making love to her with his tongue, made her hesitate.

"I'm not sure if it's a good…"

Still holding her firmly against him, Cole shook his head once. "Don't think."

"But…"

"You turned down the offer I made you the first day we met. Now I want to make you an altogether different one," he said. "Will you hear me out?"

Again, her sensible side attempted to intervene. *Get your panties off the floor, put them on and get out of here*, it implored. Sage knew she should heed the warning, but instead found herself nodding her head.

She'd simply listen to what he had to say, she reasoned. Then she'd make her excuses and leave. Just chalk up what had happened between them to a temporary lapse of judgment.

"Let's finish what we started upstairs in a big room with a huge bed."

Sage pressed her lips together to prevent an involuntary moan from escaping. She wasn't sure whether it was the persuasiveness of his deep voice or the concrete feel of him pressed against her, but she nodded her agreement.

Cole's smile lit up his entire face, mirroring how she felt inside.

"Great," he said. "Let's find the front desk and check in, so I can get busy making you my Valentine."

* * *

Cole plucked a chocolate-dipped strawberry from the silver tray on the bedside table. He held it up, just out of reach from the naked woman lying across the bed.

"You're not playing fair," Sage said. She was on her stomach, propped up by her elbows, her chin resting on her hands.

The position offered an enticing view of her cleavage and an even better one of the ass Cole couldn't keep his eyes or his hands off. "I thought you knew by now I don't play fair."

He took a big bite out of the juicy berry and slowly chewed. Sage's lips, puffy from an afternoon of his kisses, drew into a pout.

"Don't even try it with that face," he said. "You know it gets me hard."

"Everything I've done since we checked in to this suite gets you hard."

Leaning his back against the headboard, Cole polished off the strawberry. He couldn't argue. Everything about this woman turned him on. They'd made love against the door within seconds of walking through it. Mental snapshots of those stiletto boots wrapped around his waist as he drove into her again and again clicked through his mind.

Next they'd steamed up the glass-enclosed shower before finally tumbling into the king-size bed for round three.

"But I'm not complaining." Sage's faux scowl transformed into a satisfied grin.

"Stop flattering me and answer the question."

"What did you ask me, again?"

Cole selected another strawberry from the tray, this one covered in milk chocolate and candied pecans.

"Tell me." The sheet covering the lower half of his nude body shifted as he leaned forward. He brought the fruit within an inch of Sage's lips. "Was Lick Me actually the name of that lipstick?"

"What makes you doubt it?" She tried to take a bite out of the strawberry, but she didn't answer his question and he pulled it away.

"I familiarized myself with Stiletto's catalog before I made the offer to buy it," he said. "I don't remember a lipstick with that name."

"Maybe it's a new shade that we haven't officially added to the catalog yet."

"Is that the case?" Cole polished off the fruit.

Sage rose to all fours and crawled toward him. The tips of her breasts brushed his bare chest as she reached across him and grabbed a berry from the tray.

"Seeing as how you're the competition, that information is confidential." She took a bite of the juicy berry and chewed slowly. She rested her chin on his chest and pinned him with those big brown eyes.

In them, Cole saw the sweet vulnerable side he suspected she didn't often reveal. The woman could be as frustrating and challenging as she was smart and beautiful, but at this moment he found her incredibly endearing.

It was a moment he wanted to savor as he enjoyed their sexy banter.

"My question involves a yes or no, Sage. Answering it wouldn't involve spilling any of Stiletto's secrets," he said. "Besides, this afternoon is about me and you, remember?" Cole touched a finger to his chest and then to the tip of her nose. "Not Espresso. Not Stiletto."

As if on cue, a text chime sounded from Sage's purse in the other room of the suite. Her assistant had instructed the front desk to lock it in the hotel safe when she'd been unable to locate her boss. The desk clerk had returned it to Sage when they'd checked in.

The phone began to ring. Sage raised her chin from his chest and looked toward the other room.

"I meant to shut it off after I texted Amelia from the front desk," she said. "Then we came up here, and you've kept me distracted ever since."

Once they'd entered the suite, somewhere between stripping off each other's clothes and making love against the door, he and Sage had come to an unspoken agreement to leave the world outside. And there would be absolutely no discussions involving their respective businesses.

"It has to be work." She seemed torn as her eyes darted from him to the doorway separating the bedroom from the front room. "I'm just going to take a quick look and read the message. I'll be right back."

Cole instantly missed the soft warmth of her body as she left the bed and padded barefoot into the other room to retrieve her phone. The seductive sway of her round ass made him want to reach out and grab it, throw her over his shoulder and haul her back into bed.

He tempered the urge to go caveman. Where in the hell had it come from anyway? This was simply an afternoon of great sex with a woman he was wildly attracted to. *Nothing more.*

Cole told himself he was satisfied and had worked her out of his system, but the burgeoning erection on the verge of tenting the sheet was downright greedy when it came to Sage Matthews.

Sage returned to the bedroom, phone in hand. Her face wore a rare indecisive expression. "It was someone from my team wondering if..."

She began to pace as she explained the reason for the text.

Exhaling, Cole steeled himself for the disappointment of her leaving to put out some fire at Stiletto. He of all people should understand. In the past, he'd also broken it off with a woman or two who hadn't been willing to take a backseat to his job.

Yet, it niggled at him.

Not because he was hoping for another round of sex, although more of it had been on his afternoon agenda. Nor was it that he was having fun getting to know her beyond their attraction and characteristics they seemed to have in common, although, he now craved her sharp mind and quick wit as much as her body.

Then it occurred to Cole that their similarities were exactly what bothered him. During his first stint working for his mother at Espresso and then later as an executive at Force, he'd been exactly like her.

It had taken walking away from both to make him realize he couldn't do it all. Nor could he control everything. He had to trust others to help him.

Cole reached for Sage's hand. He looked pointedly at the phone in her other palm and then at her. "Just. Let. Go."

"Of my phone?" Sage's pretty face scrunched up in confusion.

Finding her naked curves a distraction, Cole rose from the bed and retrieved plush white robes from the bedroom closet. He donned the larger one, before wrapping her in the other.

"Let's talk for a moment," he said.

Cole could practically see the wheels of her brain spinning. Although they hadn't known each other long, a part of him knew her as well as he knew himself. Mentally, she was already leaping ahead to whatever work problem she presumed only she could resolve.

"But I just told you, I have to…"

"This will only take a few minutes," he said. "And who knows, I might just give you back your underwear."

The corner of her mouth quirked upward into a hint of a smile, and she nodded her agreement. Taking her by the hand, Cole led her to the sofa in the front room.

"I know it's none of my concern, but I don't think either of us can deny anymore that we're two of a kind," he said.

She looked down at their joined hands. "I tried to chalk it up to coincidence, but there have been too many now," she said. "We can both be cocky, pushy, dominating, insensitive and even a little ruthless when necessary."

"And those are probably our good points." Cole chuckled. His heart did a strange flip-flop when she squeezed his hand and laughed along.

He pressed on, although chances were she wouldn't be pleased to hear his unsolicited advice. "With that said, we're also confident, responsible, honest, hardworking and competitive. There's also no denying we're good at what we do."

Sage's brown eyes narrowed. "Those all sound like virtues to me, so why do I sense there's an impending *but*?"

"Because in excess virtues turn into liabilities."

"I'm not following you."

"Are you enjoying yourself this afternoon?" He asked.

She spared a glance at his crotch. "Immensely."

Forcing himself to remain focused on their conversation, Cole looked past her heated gaze to the phone in her free hand. "And exactly when was the last time you enjoyed yourself?" he asked, and then quickly amended. "I don't mean sex. Tell me the last time you took a couple of hours for yourself. Saw a movie? Had a massage? Read the latest bestseller? Or turned into a couch potato in front of the television?"

Cole had already known the answers to his questions, however her silence and the blank expression confirmed it.

"You're here now. Let's continue to enjoy the day and each other."

"But I have to…"

Cole saw her grip tighten around her phone. "No," he said, "*you* don't."

"I have a business to run."

He saw the spark of annoyance in her eyes and expounded before her temper ignited. "I realize that. I also realize this isn't my place, and I should stay in my lane. However, part of me feels like I know you as well as I know myself," he said. "You've got to learn you can't control everything."

Sage extricated her hand from his and huffed out a sigh. "Just what I need, another person insinuating I'm a control freak."

Cole raised a brow. "Well, aren't you, *General*?"

Sage abruptly stood. "How dare you?" she ground out, the temper he'd hoped to avoid now full-blown. "The only thing you're right about is the fact you should stay in your lane. Just who do you think you are?"

"The admiral."

"Huh?"

"The admiral," Cole repeated. "It's the name the employees who worked under me at Force Cosmetics called me behind my back."

He took advantage of Sage's surprise to continue. "Coming from my family's company, I felt like I had a lot to prove, and I went about it by being a workaholic, micromanaging control freak."

She sat back on the sofa, and once again, Cole took her hand in his.

"I earned that moniker and probably a lot worse. Along with the disgruntlement of the people who worked for me," he said. "I was never locked in a closet, but only because they never got the opportunity."

They shared a private smile, and Cole could feel the tension melt between them and her anger ebb away. Sage stared down at the phone in her hand.

"Stiletto's more than just a business to me, it's…" She started, paused, and then started again. "Even if I wanted to, I'm not sure I can stop being the general."

"Were all of Stiletto's hiring decisions made by you?" He asked.

Sage nodded.

"Are you confident in your judgment?"

Again, she nodded.

"Then trust your decision and the people you hired to do their jobs. Take the first step." Cole pulled his hand from hers and placed it over the one holding the phone. *"Delegate."*

Her watched her gnaw at her bottom lip as she stared at his hand covering the phone.

"I'm not sure if you can understand this, but I'm not talking about surrendering control of your business. I'm talking about freeing yourself of the minutiae so you can truly take control of it." Cole patted her hand and rose from the sofa. "Now I'm going back to the bedroom to enjoy those delicious strawberries while I persuade Burger Tower to deliver. I hope you'll decide to stay and join me."

Cole hoped like hell she would. Deep down he didn't expect her to. With every step back to the suite's bedroom and the sex-rumpled bed they'd shared, he prepared to watch her get dressed and leave.

Ten minutes later, Cole was sitting on the bed scrolling through Burger Town's menu on his phone's web browser. He looked up to find Sage standing in the doorway. She was holding her own phone to her ear.

"Yes, you heard right. I want you to do what I hired you to do and handle it," she said into the phone.

Their eyes connected across the room. When she smiled, Cole's chest tightened with an emotion he couldn't identify.

"If there's anything else, contact Amelia," Sage said, the phone still against her ear. "I'm unavailable for the rest of the day."

She shut off the phone and tossed it over her shoulder. He laughed as she made a running dive for the bed. Sage landed on top of him, and Cole finally pinpointed the emotion blooming inside of him. *Happiness.*

"By the way, the answer to your question is no," she said.

"Huh?" He was so relieved she'd decided to stay that he had no idea what she was talking about.

"Earlier, you asked if my lipstick shade was really called Lick Me." Her smile turned seductive as she slowly shook her head. "The answer is *no.*"

In an instant, Cole was harder than he'd ever been in his life. "Mind telling me the actual name?"

"Not at all." Sage rose to her knees on the bed and shed the hotel robe. She leaned in and whispered the name of the lipstick shade in his ear.

He faced her. "Really?"

"Really," she confirmed.

Cole flung his phone across the room in the vicinity of hers and pulled her into his arms. "Well, let's see if we're both flexible enough to make that happen."

Chapter 12

The next day, Sage stood in her bedroom staring at her reflection in the full-length mirror.

It was a good thing Amelia wasn't around. She would have noticed the flush in Sage's cheeks, the extra sparkle in her eyes and the fact she was practically glowing—and blown it totally out of proportion.

Her assistant would have immediately jumped to conclusions and likened her to a heroine in one of those sappy romance novels.

"It was just good sex," Sage told her reflection as she as she switched her hoop earrings for black pearl studs. "Nothing more."

Her explanation disregarded the fact that the afternoon she'd spent with Cole had extended into the evening and then overnight. It overlooked that she was expecting him to pick her up any minute now for dinner.

She shoved her feet into a pair of gray patent-leather

combat boots, grateful to have a respite from her usual heels. She wore a gray minidress with matching tights. Cole had said he was taking her somewhere casual and there was no need to dress up.

Cole.

Sage smiled at the thought of seeing him again. Catching sight of her face in the mirror, she wiped the grin off her face.

They were simply having dinner together. Tomorrow morning, they'd return to the real world, sit behind desks at their respective businesses and resume being competitors. However, for the remainder of the weekend they were friends and *lovers*.

The doorbell rang. Sage sucked in a big gulp of air and exhaled to quell her excitement at seeing him again.

Good Lord, she'd just seen the man an hour ago. If she didn't keep herself in check, she would indeed be as bad as Amelia.

Sage opened the door and the grin returned to her face. Cole stood in the doorway. He wore wool pants and a sweater topped by a black leather jacket. She looked from his gray slacks and sweater to her own gray attire and shuddered.

"We're so much alike it can be downright spooky," she said.

He wrapped an arm around her, pulled her against him and kissed her. "I'm a lot more interested in our differences." His hand slid down to her behind. "Namely this gorgeous ass and those endless legs of yours."

Sage kissed him again, and then inclined her head toward the inside of her house. "Come in, before the neighbors see me throwing myself at you."

Sage hadn't had many visitors, just the family next door or Amelia, who occasionally stopped by for something related to Stiletto. As she led Cole inside, it occurred to her how modest the small cottage she took so much pride in must look to someone of his wealth and background.

"Nice house." His tone was genuine as he looked around her living room with its repurposed furniture and kitschy decor. "When things settle down at Espresso, I'm thinking of buying in this part of town."

"Really?" Sage couldn't keep the note of surprise out of her voice. Although it was rapidly changing, the neighborhood was still considered rough by most.

"Sure. Not only is it a great investment in an up-and-coming area, it's walkable, has a sense of community, as well as great restaurants," he said. "I'm always coming here to eat anyway."

Sage nodded. Those reasons along with her budget were the same reasons she'd settled here.

"Right now, I live in a town house I bought a few years after college, but I never took time to really make it a home. Not like this."

Again, Sage found herself taken aback that he appeared to see her house the same way she did. She was also surprised at where he lived.

"By the look on your face, I'm guessing you thought I resided in some mega mansion south of the city," Cole said.

Sage nodded. It had been exactly what she'd thought. It was also one of the two areas people with substantial wealth put down roots.

"My town house has an entire floor I'm rarely in." He shrugged. "It seemed excessive for me to buy a huge house to live in alone."

Remembering her manners, she offered him a seat and a drink.

Cole glanced at his watch. "We'd better get going if we want to be on time for dinner."

Assuming he'd made reservations at a nearby restaurant, Sage shrugged on her red coat and grabbed her purse. She hadn't eaten since Cole had ordered breakfast in bed from hotel room service that morning, and it was now nearly six.

Locking her front door, she saw his car parked behind hers in the driveway and did a double take at the black Dodge Challenger, which, except for the color, was identical to her red one. Sage looked up at Cole. "Again, spooky."

"Or perhaps it's kismet," he said softly.

Sage brushed off his words and the little piece of her heart they touched with a casual shrug. As Cole drove, she wasn't sure if it was the familiarity of the car or the similarities they shared, but she felt close to the man. They'd only seen each other a few times, but in some ways it was as if she'd known him her entire life.

Now who's the one being ridiculous? the commonsense part of her that often mocked Amelia questioned.

Caught up in her thoughts, Sage hadn't paid attention to where they were going until the car slowed along the cul-de-sac of a residential street.

"I thought we were going to a restaurant," she said.

Cole turned into the driveway of a two-story, Craftsman-style home. "I said I wanted to have dinner with you, but if I miss another invite to my aunt's for Sunday dinner she'll kill me," he said. "I didn't want to disappoint her. Also, I want to make the most of this time with you before we both return to work in the morning."

He didn't say it, but they both knew their obligations to their businesses overshadowed any feelings they thought they had for each other.

"You should have told me dinner was with your family," she said.

"I was afraid you'd say no."

Cole was right, of course—she would have. His family was powerful and wealthy, and Sage didn't like putting herself in the position of feeling like the poor, orphaned girl.

He reached over the console and grasped her hand. "I apologize for not telling you," he said. "If it'll make you feel better, my cousins are all girls so I'll be outnumbered."

Sage softened to the idea. "Well…"

"You'll like them and my aunt Janet," Cole said.

Sage nodded her agreement. In college, she'd dated guys from rich backgrounds, one seriously. None of them were eager to bring a woman who lacked both money and connections around their relatives. Yet Cole, a man who could buy the lot of them ten times over, was practically pleading with her to meet his family.

"Still, I wish I'd known. I would have brought flowers or a bottle of wine," she said.

"All you need to bring is yourself." Cole squeezed her hand. "That's plenty." He leaned over the car's console and kissed her.

Sage sighed into his mouth, swept away by the slow dance of his tongue mingling with hers. The man's panty-melting kisses would be the first thing she missed when they resumed their lives tomorrow.

A knock on the driver's side window startled them, and they broke apart, ending the kiss.

"Put it on pause. The rest of us would like to eat sometime this evening."

Sage looked from Cole's wide smile through the window to a woman standing by the car. She had honey-hued skin and shoulder-length sandy-brown dreadlocks. Her hands were fisted on her hips, but her warm smile matched the one on Cole's face.

He rounded the car and held the door open for her.

"Sage Matthews meet my rude cousin, Riley Sinclair," he said. His fondness of his cousin permeated his voice.

The woman raised a brow. "*The* Sage Matthews?"

"The very one," Cole said.

"Nice to meet you," Riley said. "Although after yesterday, I expected all I'd see of you was your foot in my cousin's…"

"Riley!" Cole scolded.

Sage stifled a laugh at the interplay between the two.

"My crew and I were responsible for transforming the hotel's Grand Ballroom into Espresso's makeover central yesterday," Riley said. "Hope you won't hold that against me."

"I won't," Sage confirmed, taking an instant liking to Riley Sinclair. "However, I will take your card just in case I need you to help me construct a little payback."

Cole's cousin slapped her on the back. Sage stumbled and nearly saw stars, the woman's friendly gesture packing quite a wallop.

"We'd better get inside. Mom's about ready to put dinner on the table," Riley said.

Cole's hand rested lightly on her back as Sage followed his cousin up the porch stairs and into the house. The place had the same warm, inviting vibe as Riley. Its open floor plan provided unobstructed views of both the living room and the dining room table, which was already set for dinner.

A woman who appeared to be in her midsixties fussed over the table. Her entire face lit up the moment she spotted Cole. She put down the napkin she was folding, rushed over and enveloped him in a huge hug.

"Glad to see you could make it to dinner." The older woman beamed up at him. "I thought I was going to have to send Riley after you."

"I wouldn't miss having dinner with my favorite aunt."

His aunt swatted his arm, and then turned to Sage. "And I'm even more delighted to see you've brought your girl-friend," she said. "Maybe she'll keep you here in Nash-ville, and you won't take off again, gallivanting all over the world."

"Oh, I'm not his girlfriend," Sage said automatically.

The older woman dismissed her claim with a wave of her hand. "Of course you are, hon. Why else would you have spent the past fifteen minutes in the driveway, steam-ing up my nephew's car windows?" she asked sweetly. Then she added a mischievous wink that made her look like her daughter.

"Aunt Janet, I'd like you to meet my *friend*, Sage Mat-thews," he said. "She also runs a cosmetics company here in town."

"Riley's already filled me in on the particulars," the older woman said.

"Nice to meet you, Mrs. Sinclair." Sage extended her hand.

The woman bypassed Sage's outstretched hand. Instead, she wrapped her in a hug as warm as the one she'd be-stowed on her nephew. Cole had been right. She liked both his aunt and his cousin, and Sage suspected she'd feel the same about his other cousins.

"So where are Nina and Hope?" Cole asked, looking around.

"Nina's on a job in Memphis, and Hope's home sick," Janet called over her shoulder on the way to the kitchen.

"It's just a cold," Riley said. "I took some chicken soup over to her place earlier."

Soon the four of them were seated at the dining room table. The conversation was minimal as they dug into a Sunday dinner consisting of a juicy rotisserie chicken, salad, macaroni and cheese, mashed potatoes, and warm cornbread muffins smothered in sweet honey butter.

Good food overwhelmed the rules of etiquette and Sage was the first to ask for seconds, soon joined by both Cole and Riley.

"I don't mean to be rude, but unless my next door neighbor takes pity on me I don't sit down to a home-cooked meal often," Sage said, heaping another scoop of mashed potatoes onto her plate.

Janet and her daughter exchanged glances.

"Actually, you aren't sitting down to one this evening, either," Cole's aunt said. "Like most of my meals, this one was picked up ready-made at the grocery store."

"Sage isn't the only one who thought this was home-made. I thought you'd spent all day in the kitchen," Cole said, reaching for more chicken.

Janet Sinclair took a sip from her water glass and placed it back on the table. "Like you two, I have a business to oversee. Sinclair Construction doesn't run itself." The older woman inclined her head toward the kitchen. "So that stove in there is for looking—not for cooking."

Both Cole and Sage smiled, while Riley snorted. "That's no great culinary loss," she said. "Even before Dad died and you took over Sinclair Construction, anything you *cooked* came frozen on a plastic tray and accompanied by the beep of the microwave."

Janet shot her daughter a faux dirty look, which collapsed into laughter. "True," she admitted.

The older woman turned her attention to Sage. "We already know how Cole ended up in the cosmetics game," she said. "How about you? What prompted you to get in the beauty business?"

"My mother," Sage answered.

In her peripheral vision she could see Cole put down his fork and turn to her.

"Mom worked at a department-store makeup counter," she continued. "As a single parent, she simply couldn't afford to get me the dolls, games and toys kids all want. So she'd bring home samples of gorgeous lipsticks, blushes and eye shadow for me to play with and somehow managed to turn makeup into my absolute favorite game."

Janet nodded approvingly. "Your mother must be very proud of your accomplishments."

"I'd like think she is," Sage said. "She died when I was eleven, and I grew up in foster care."

"Oh, dear," the older woman said. "I'm sorry."

Sage nodded. She was facing Janet and Riley; however, her next words were meant for Cole more so than his family. "I do what I do to honor her memory, which makes Stiletto more than just a business to me. It's more than just my dream. It was my mother's dream for me."

She turned to Cole. More than merely their gazes connected. It made her feel closer to him in that moment than they had been in bed.

"So what made you decide to set up a cosmetics company in Nashville of all places instead of New York?" Riley asked.

The connection broken, Sage blinked and focused on Cole's cousin's question. "The internet makes it possible for me to anchor my business wherever I want, so I decided to stay in my hometown. I like it here, plus I can plow more money into the business because I don't have the overhead of maintaining a pricey Manhattan address."

Cole chimed in. "My mother often said it gave her the first pick of Tennessee State's and Fisk's new graduates."

"That, too," Sage said. "My advertising manager, Joe

Archer, is a Fisk graduate, and I'm a Tennessee State alumnus."

"So is Mom," Riley said.

Janet nodded. "I earned my teaching degree at TSU, but that was way before your time."

"Sage's undergrad degree is in chemistry, and she also has an MBA," Cole said. Sage could hear the note of pride in his voice.

It made her feel good.

Janet and her daughter exchanged glances.

"Oh, I picked up dessert at the grocery store, too," Cole's aunt said. "Anyone up for apple pie?"

"Of course, you know it's my absolute favorite, Aunt Janet."

He touched Sage's hand under the table, a question in his eyes.

She nodded and smiled at him. "It's my absolute favorite dessert, too."

Sage wasn't sure how long they sat staring at each other, goofy grins pasted on their faces. Janet cleared her throat, and Sage abruptly snatched her hand back. The cutlery clanked against the plates as her hand hit the underside of the table.

"Sage, honey, I was wondering if you would help me clear the table and give me a hand in the kitchen with coffee and dessert," Janet said. "Riley, I believe you had something to talk over with Cole."

"Um, sure." Sage rose from the table and began gathering plates and silverware.

Cole's cousin launched into a conversation about blueprints and Espresso's building as Sage followed Janet into the kitchen. She figured the older woman wanted to get the competition out of earshot so the two cousins could talk business.

Once they were in the kitchen, Sage began the task of scraping the plates over the trash can so she could load them into the dishwasher. Janet stopped her. "Leave it— my housekeeper will take care of it when he arrives in the morning."

Cole's aunt gestured toward a padded bar stool in front of the huge granite-topped kitchen island. The apple pie was already atop the island along with four dessert plates "Have a seat." Janet retrieved a knife. "You can slice the pie while I make coffee."

It was now apparent to Sage that the older woman's underlying purpose hadn't been to get her out of the dining room so Cole and Riley could discuss the Espresso building. Sage slid off the bar stool, washed her hands at the double sink and dried them with a paper towel.

Returning to the kitchen island, she picked up the knife and cut into the pie. "So exactly what do you want to talk to me about, ma'am?"

"You're direct," Cole's aunt said.

"I try to be," Sage said.

"Good for you. I see why my nephew's so taken with you."

Sage sighed. The older woman was jumping to all the wrong conclusions, but after she'd seen her and Cole steaming up the car windows, it wouldn't be easy to dissuade her.

Janet filled a carafe with water and poured it into the coffeemaker. "Cole's always so serious. Ever since he was a boy," she said. "I don't think I've ever seen him smile as much as I have tonight, and you're the reason."

Sage kept her mouth shut. It wasn't as if she could explain that being sexed up for nearly twenty-four hours was the real reason behind her nephew's smile.

"I'm not one for interfering in my girls' or Cole's lives,

but the last time he was hurt, he took a job out of the country. Both he and his sisters were tight-lipped about it. He didn't even confide in Riley, but I do know he was heartbroken." Cole's aunt added a scoopful of coffee to the coffeemaker and switched it on. She pulled mugs from a cherrywood cabinet. "I love my nephew, and I like having him back in town."

"Look, Mrs. Sinclair, I'm not exactly sure where you're going with this, but you've got it all wrong. Cole and I are not a couple."

The older woman faced Sage, a skeptical expression on her face. "As a mother of three who's been in business for nearly twenty years, frankly, that doesn't pass my internal bullshit detector."

Cole's aunt took advantage of Sage's surprise at her language and continued.

"I'm not blind. I saw the way he looks at you. I also see the way you look at him. I don't care what you two are calling your relationship, all I'm asking is you keep that smile on my nephew's face. I like having Cole in town, and I like seeing him happy."

Sage knew it was futile trying to convince the woman there was no relationship. Whatever she and Cole had this weekend would end the moment they each arrived at work tomorrow morning.

"You okay?"

Seated in Cole's car, they asked the question simultaneously.

Their moods had shifted over dessert. While they both continued to nod, speak or laugh at the appropriate times, Cole had noticed Sage seemed distracted. So was he.

The short discussion with his cousin about the Espresso building had put a lot on his mind. He and his sisters had pretty much decided to sell it. Although the three of them could easily overrule Victor's vote in the matter, they'd been trying to give him time to adjust to the idea.

Now Cole wasn't so sure selling it was the answer. Riley's alternative plan had intrigued him.

Waving out the window at his aunt and cousin, Cole backed the Challenger out of his aunt's driveway. He spared a glance at the passenger seat as he pressed the button to close the window.

"I hope Aunt Janet didn't grill you too badly while you two were in the kitchen."

"Not at all," Sage said. "However, I did spend most of the time trying to convince her we aren't together. I don't think she believes me."

Because maybe we should be together, Cole thought. And this was the perfect opening to say so.

"She missed me while I was away and has been a touch overprotective since my return," he said aloud. Inwardly, he kicked himself for blowing an opportunity to tell her he wished this weekend could be more than just a one-time occurrence.

Cole wanted it to be a beginning.

"She says you left Nashville over a broken heart," Sage said.

Cole's grip on the steering wheel tightened as he steered the car through the quiet residential streets leading to the expressway. Sage was unwittingly inching toward a matter he didn't discuss, with anyone.

"I guess you could say that," he said finally. That much was true. He had been heartbroken. "However, it had nothing to do with a romantic relationship."

His body remained tense as he braced himself for her to press the issue. In his experience, women rarely took things at face value. They had to delve into and explore every emotion, instead of just letting it be.

"Anyway, I think both your aunt and your cousin are great."

Instead of relentless questions, Sage had changed the subject. It was all Cole could do not to pull the car to the side of the road and kiss her. Tension ebbed away from his shoulders as he merged onto the expressway.

"I envy you for having a family that cares so much about you," she continued.

Cole heard the hint of wistfulness in her tone. Without stopping to think about it, he reached across the console separating the car's bucket seats for her hand.

"I do consider myself fortunate to have them." He'd gleaned from interviews he'd read about Sage that she had spent the majority of her childhood in foster care. "However, it doesn't keep me from sometimes feeling like I'm on the outside looking in."

He could feel her gaze on him as he drove.

"But, why?" she asked.

"Riley and my cousins lost their father, but still have Aunt Janet. My sisters and I lost our mother, but they still have my stepfather, Victor," Cole said. He released her hand, so he could signal before changing lanes. "Being the one with no parents makes me feel like the odd orphan out at times. If that makes any sense."

Cole had never admitted it aloud before. At thirty-four years old, he probably shouldn't give it a thought. However, occasionally it made him feel incredibly alone. His mother was gone, and all he'd had to know his father ever existed were old photos and the worn Timex he'd worn on his wrist.

Cole felt Sage's hand on his thigh. Its warmth penetrated the fabric of his wool pants, the gesture touching him deeper than words.

It also made him sad the weekend was rapidly coming to an end.

All too soon, Cole turned into Sage's driveway and parked behind her red Challenger. He didn't shut off the car engine and was relieved when she didn't immediately jump out of the car.

Her sigh filled the car's silent cabin. "As badly as I want to invite you in for the night, I don't think it's a good idea," she said. "It'll only make it that much harder to put an end to this in the morning."

It was hard now, he thought. Cole couldn't explain it to her. Hell, he couldn't explain it to himself. All he knew was he wanted to see more of her—both in and out of the bedroom.

"I have something I want you to think over," Cole said.

"Another offer?" She stared out the windshield.

He chuckled lightly, feeling more nervous than he had the day he asked the homecoming queen to the prom. "Something like that," he said. "I have a trip scheduled and will be leaving later this week. However, while I'm gone, I'd like you to think about us going out on a date when I return."

"B-but…" she began.

However, Cole wasn't done. Reaching across the console, he used his finger to turn her head until she faced him. "Believe me, I know as well as you do all the reasons we shouldn't," he said. "Still, I want to take you on a real date. Hold your hand in a movie. Buy you a milkshake and the biggest burger in town. Or cook dinner for you at my place and afterward make love to you in my bed."

The dim light of the car's controls softly illuminated

her face. A face he hoped to see more of when he returned from Milan.

"All I need you to do tonight is promise you'll think about it," he said finally.

Sage nodded. "I promise."

A promise Cole hoped would lead to the opportunity for him to win her heart.

Chapter 13

After their sabotaged Valentine's Day event, Sage hadn't expected the positive updates coming from her team at Monday morning's staff meeting.

She should have been overjoyed. Instead, she stifled a yawn.

"So while Espresso's horning in on us might have ended our event sooner than we would have liked, social media–wise, it was a success."

While Stiletto's social media manager droned on in the background, Sage reached for one of the two thermal carafes on the conference room table. She poured herself a second mug of black coffee and took a generous gulp.

It wouldn't replace the sleep she'd missed the night before, tossing, turning and longing for Cole. However, Sage hoped a caffeine jolt would give her enough energy to get through the remainder of the morning along with a dose of much-needed focus.

"Our invitees had no idea our party was being upstaged by Espresso. From their social media posts, it appears everyone believed it was a joint event," the social media head said.

Sage forced herself to concentrate as the woman continued to fill everyone in on her findings, including complimentary videos and blog posts by the notorious Wicked Glam Mother and other attendees. Normally, Sage would have been riveted.

However, the only thing on her mind was the promise she'd made to Cole last night. The irony wasn't lost on her. He'd only asked her to think about going on a date with him. Now the man was *all* she could think about—his hands, his lips, his tongue all over her body.

"So what do you think?" Joe Archer asked.

The question roused Sage from her reverie to the expectant faces awaiting her answer.

"Sorry, I was thinking about an idea for our Christmas collection," Sage fibbed. "Could you repeat what you said?"

She stifled another yawn, drawing a curious look from Amelia. Sage avoided her assistant's assessing gaze. Taking another gulp from her coffee mug, she directed her attention to Stiletto's head of advertising.

"I think it's a fantastic opportunity for Stiletto, but I know you like to manage these things," he said. The subtle emphasis he put on the word *manage* made it sound like the word she suspected he wanted to use was *micromanage*.

Again, Cole popped into her head. Not the escalating battle of one-upmanship between their companies or the similarities they continued to discover about one another, but the man who respected her enough as a businesswoman to offer his advice.

I'm not talking about surrendering control of your busi-

*ness. I'm talking about freeing yourself from the minutiae
so you can truly take control of it.*

Cole's melodic baritone slipped into her head as if he'd
just taken a seat beside her. Sage fisted her hands against
the resistance rising up in her. When her mother died, so
much had been out of her control that she couldn't help trying to dominate every detail of the company she'd created.

It had been easier to loosen the reins a bit, back at the
hotel on Saturday, with the delicious options of Burger
Tower and a naked Cole as a reward.

Trust the people you hired to do their jobs. Delegate.

Deep down, she knew Cole was right. Sage had also
observed that his aunt Janet farmed out routine tasks like
cooking and cleaning. She'd said it gave her the time and
energy to be more effective at work.

Sage closed her eyes briefly. *You can do this*, she
thought. *Do it so you can make Stiletto even better.* She
cleared her throat.

"I trust your judgment, Joe," she said. "If it has your
seal of approval, then it has mine."

The conference room fell silent except for the ticking
of the clock on the wall. Anyone walking in would think
they'd stepped into the middle of a Saturday-morning cartoon where every character's eyes bulged out of their sock-
ets in exaggerated amazement.

"P-pardon?" Joe stammered. "I don't think I heard you
correctly."

"Yes, you did," Sage assured him.

She gave herself a mental pat on the back. She wasn't
sure if it was because she was proud of herself or if it was
the caffeine finally kicking in, but she suddenly felt more
energetic than she had all morning.

"Okay, next up, Shelia." Sage looked pointedly at the

woman seated next to Joe. "What do you have to say for yourself after Saturday?"

The young woman's eyes darted uncomfortably around the conference table as she picked up her notes. Both her hands and her voice trembled as she read from them.

Sage drummed her fingertips lightly against the table and watched her squirm. While she hadn't been able to pinpoint the voices of the employees who'd locked her in the linen closet, she had a pretty good idea who had been involved.

"Um…I'm writing personalized thank-you notes to include with the mini–lipstick samplers we're sending out this week." A fine sheen of perspiration covered the woman's forehead as she continued to stammer through her update.

Sage had been sweating herself when she'd first arrived at the office. The general vibe of the office and lack of commentary from Amelia had assured her that while everyone had heard about her being locked in the hotel's linen closet—they hadn't an inkling of what had actually gone down in the closet.

Her captors hadn't seen Cole walk in before her, and fortunately both events had ended by the time the hotel employee freed them.

Sage suppressed a shiver at the memory of Cole in the closet as well as later in the hotel suite.

She returned her attention to Shelia, who had finally wrapped up her update. "Is that it?" Sage asked, narrowing her gaze. "Are you sure there isn't something else you'd like to tell me?"

"Uh…no. That was all I had." Shelia's voice was still shaky. It possessed none of the rancor it had back in the hotel ladies' room.

Sage hoped she was having flashbacks of scooping up hot buttered grits at the Waffle House.

"Okay, then." Sage addressed the entire staff as their weekly meeting drew to a close. "As you know, I leave for Milan midweek. Do good work while I'm away, and Amelia can contact me if needed."

Back in her office, Sage sank into the chair behind her desk. Her assistant followed her into the office and pushed the door closed.

"So are you planning to eventually let Shelia and her closet cohorts off the hook?" Amelia pulled her phone from her pocket prepared to type in a notation if necessary. "Or should I begin reviewing résumés to find their replacements?"

Sage opened her mouth to answer, and then another thought occurred to her. "Exactly when did you find out they'd locked me up?"

"Not until this morning, when I heard them talking about it. What seemed like a wonderful idea two days ago now has them shaking in their pumps, expecting pink slips." Her assistant shrugged. "Anyway, when I couldn't find you, I figured you and Freddy Finch were somewhere in the hotel torturing Cole Sinclair, because I didn't see the two of them around, either."

Again, Sage was grateful Amelia had no inkling where she'd been, what she'd been doing and whom she had been doing it with. The young woman had been insufferable enough after she'd walked in on her and Cole kissing.

"I was hoping to snag one of those gorgeous centerpieces your neighbor made for myself, but our guests took them as souvenirs," Amelia continued.

"Evie did a great job," Sage agreed. "I'm hoping this encourages her to start her own business."

Rolling her chair closer to her desk, Sage tapped a finger on her computer's keyboard to rouse it from sleep mode.

"You haven't said what your plans are for Shelia and her coconspirators." Amelia raised a hand. "I know what they did is insubordination and a firing offense by any boss's standard. However, in their defense, you were a bit of a pill on Saturday, General, even more than usual. It was like watching a Valentine's Day version of *How the Grinch Stole Christmas*." Her assistant rolled her eyes. "I was seconds away from locking you up and throwing away the key myself."

Sage checked her watch, and then drummed her fingertips against the desktop. "Are you nearly ready to rest your case, because I have a lot of work to do before I leave for Milan?"

Amelia sighed. "I'm guessing you've already made up your mind."

She'd decided their fate before she'd come to work this morning. "They're good at their jobs, and I have no intention of firing them over a momentary lapse in judgment."

Her assistant froze, and her phone slipped from her grasp. She bent over to retrieve it. "So you're going to let it go, just like that?"

"Yep, just like that." Sage confirmed, looking at her computer monitor. "It's minutia. I need to reserve my energy to remain focused on the big picture." She'd enjoyed watching Shelia squirm this morning, but it was time to get back to business.

"What's gotten into you?"

Wouldn't you like to know. Sage kept the thought to herself, and her eyes fixed on her computer screen.

Amelia snorted. "Whatever it was, I hope you get a lot more of it."

* * *

A knock sounded on Cole's closed office door, and Loretta walked through it.

"Your next appointment is here," she said.

Cole looked away from the mood board Espresso's creative department had prepared with proposed ideas and color swatches for next year's spring collection. He exhaled. "You can show her...I mean *him* in."

"Do you need me to stick around to referee?" A gravelly grunt accompanied his secretary's question.

"Is he dressed like the Espresso Granny?"

Damn. Cole ground his teeth together. How was he supposed to convince the makeup-buying public the man had no association with Espresso when, thanks to Sage, he was starting to buy into it himself?

Sage. The thought of her and the stunt she'd pulled at the hotel should have left him angry. However, spending the remainder of the weekend with her made it seem as though it had happened a lifetime ago. He hoped when he returned from Milan there would be more weekends together in their future.

"Looks like Mr. Finch left his granny getup at home today," Loretta said.

"Go ahead and send him in," Cole said. "I'll yell if I need you to pry my fingers from around his throat."

Seconds later, Freddy Finch stepped hesitantly into his office. "Um, you wanted to see me."

Without the dress, wig and makeup, Finch appeared to be in his early twenties, Cole observed. Tall and lanky, he bore little resemblance to the overweight old crone he portrayed.

Cole walked away from the mood board set up on an easel. He took in Finch's threadbare jeans, old sneakers and worn Tennessee Titans jersey bearing the number of a player who'd retired a decade ago.

"Thanks for coming, Mr. Finch." He gestured to the chair in front of his desk. "Have a seat."

Freddy eyed the chair suspiciously before sitting down. "Hey, man, I don't want any trouble."

"I'm sure you don't." Rounding his desk, Cole sat in his own chair. As usual, he got right to the point. "Here's my problem, you dressing up as the so-called Espresso Granny is negatively impacting my company."

The young man shrugged. "The newspaper photo shoot and gigs I did for Stiletto were just to help me keep a roof over my head until my drag queen show takes off. My folks kicked me out, when I dropped out of college to pursue it full-time," he said. "Things are picking up, but it's been rough."

Cole let the young man rattle on about his song-and-dance routine for a few minutes before he stopped him. "Let's get down to the reason I asked you here."

"If you're going to sue me, you should know up-front I don't have anything."

That much was obvious, Cole thought. However, he had an alternate idea. If Finch agreed to it, Cole believed it might be a solution to both of their problems.

"Mr. Finch. I want to offer you a job."

Sweat broke out on the man's shaved head. "I don't know," he said, nervously. "The last job I took from Ms. Matthews nearly got my behind kicked the other day."

Leaning back in his chair, Cole crossed his arms over his chest. "I assure you the only thing this job will get you is well paid," he said. "Oh, and it just might help get that drag queen career of yours off the ground. Interested?"

He was interested all right, Cole thought.

"I'll take it." Eagerness replaced the anxiety that had creased the young man's features just moments ago.

"But you haven't even heard what you'll be required to do."

"Doesn't matter." Finch shrugged. "If it'll keep me from having to crawl back to my folks and boost my career, too, count me in, Mr. Sinclair."

Cole quickly outlined the job with Freddy Finch nodding in agreement at every requirement. "So you'll have to don your Espresso Granny outfit one last time," he said. "Then that's the last I ever want to see of it."

Again, the young man readily agreed.

"Great. My lawyers will have the contracts to you later this afternoon." Cole knew the kid needed the money sooner rather than later and would instruct his attorney to expedite the funds. "You'll receive your first check the moment you sign them."

Finch extended his hand, and Cole shook it, sealing the verbal agreement. "I can't thank you enough, Mr. Sinclair. You idea might just turn me into a headliner."

The young man rose to leave, but Cole gestured for him to wait. He picked up the phone on his desk and punched in a number. "Hey, Max. Is Tia available?"

Seconds later, his sister's burly assistant had her on the line. After welcoming her home from her belated honeymoon and inquiring about his brother-in-law, Ethan, Cole filled Tia in on what he needed and then asked for her help.

"That's correct, a head-to-toe makeover," he confirmed. "I also need you to handle this one personally."

"I don't know." His sister hedged. "I've never done a makeover like this before. It would definitely be a challenge."

"I know I'm asking for a miracle here, sis," Cole said. "But if there's anyone who can pull this off, it's you."

When the brief call ended, Freddy left the office with an all-day appointment set for the next day at Espresso Sanctuary's flagship spa.

Cole couldn't help feeling pleased with himself as he leaned back in his chair and propped his feet on his desk. Not only had he diffused the Espresso Granny problem, he just might be able to use it to his advantage.

Chapter 14

Sage awoke with a start as the wheels of the plane bumped along the runway before skidding to a stop at Milan's Malpensa airport.

"Benvenuti a Milano," a flight attendant said over the loudspeaker.

Sage yawned and stretched her arms over her head, but the movement did little to relieve the kinks the cramped economy-class seat had left in her back and neck.

The flight attendant announced the local time, seven o'clock in the morning. Sage stifled a second yawn with her fist. It meant she'd netted exactly twenty minutes of sleep during the entire fourteen-hour journey.

Much like her life, her plan to doze the entire overnight flight had been upended by Cole Sinclair. Images and thoughts of him had greeted her each time she'd closed her eyes. Being drawn to him, being infuriated by him, being kissed by him and finally being held by him as he made love to her deep into the night.

Sage sighed and peered out of the tiny window as the plane taxied to the terminal. Only days had passed since she'd last seen Cole, but she missed him. He'd lived in Milan during his stint at Force Cosmetics. Sage couldn't help wishing she would be seeing this incredible city with him as her companion instead of a paperback travel guide.

Girl, please, her inner voice heckled as she quickly made her way through customs with only a carry-on bag for the short trip. *You want him, all right, but not for playing tour guide.*

Sage tried to force thoughts of Cole from her mind as she slid into the backseat of a white taxi. She was in Milan during fashion week, and this afternoon she had a front-row seat to view the runway show of one of Italy's most iconic fashion brands. It certainly wasn't the time or place to be moping over a man she'd only known a few weeks. They hadn't even been out on a real date.

She stared out the taxi window at the gray skies as the city came into view. Then why did it feel as if she'd known Cole for a lifetime? she wondered. Moreover, why was she starting to think Amelia's belief in romance and finding true love might not be so far-fetched after all?

Removing her city guide from her bag, Sage covered a yawn with her fist. She flipped through the pages she'd highlighted during the flight, determined to shift her focus off Cole and onto enjoying her trip and rare time away from Stiletto.

The guidebook had noted the northern Italian city was a hub for business and lacked the monuments, picturesque piazzas and stunning views of the Mediterranean offered by the country's tourist destinations. Still, Sage had a short list of things she'd hoped to do while she was in town. She wanted to see the gothic cathedral known as the Duomo di Milano, tour the museum at the Teatro alla Scala opera house and buy a pair of kick-ass designer boots along the fashion capital's real attraction, the world-renowned Golden Quadrilateral.

"Scusi, signorina. Signorina."

Startled, Sage blinked and looked out the window. The taxi was parked at her hotel. She glanced at the open guidebook on lap and concluded she'd drifted off.

Sage yawned again. Sleepiness and jet lag overwhelmed her excitement as she counted out the euros to pay the driver and checked into her hotel. She'd intended to take a shower and spend the remainder of the morning sightseeing before Marie Bertelli's driver arrived to whisk her to this afternoon's runway show.

Instead, she spent her first hours in Italy snoring beneath the duvet of her room's full-size bed.

Cole observed the crowd filing into the courtyard of Sforzesco Castle. Huge white tents, winding red carpets and endless media trucks had temporarily transformed the centuries-old fortress into the city's weeklong fashion hub as well as the venue for the Bertelli runway show.

He'd attended fashion shows during Milan's fashion week in the past and had expected to see the requisite gaggle of fashion magazine editors, bone thin and dressed head to toe in black. However, the rest of the crowd looked like a virtual who's who of headline makers from across the globe.

Cole inclined his head at the CEO of a German department store chain he'd become acquainted with during his Force Cosmetics stint. He recognized a smattering of American television reality-show stars, all famous for being famous, as well as last year's best-actor Oscar winner, who had passed out on stage in the middle of a drunken acceptance speech.

An uneasy feeling came over Cole. Not for the first time, he wondered why Marie had issued him the personal invite.

The only news he'd generated lately was a footnote in that god-awful article in *America Today* where that so-called Espresso Granny had made her, rather *his*, debut.

Cole rarely second-guessed himself. The main reason he'd decided to help Marie out with his presence was his fondness for her grandparents. However, he was starting to regret having made this trip. His time would have been better spent back in Nashville overseeing his own family's business, he thought. Although deep down he knew it wasn't his office at the Espresso building he longed for right now.

Cole wanted to be at the front door of Sage's cottage doing everything in his power to convince her to see him again.

Sage.

Damn, he missed her, entirely too much for a woman he'd only slept with one night. He'd thought about her nearly every moment of the long flight, her business savvy, her sass, the all-consuming passion she displayed both in and out of the bedroom.

Cole exhaled. He'd only been here a day, and already, he was considering shaving a few days off the trip. He'd arrived in Milan yesterday morning, rented a car and driven directly to his condo. The cleaner who came in once a month to maintain his place, which occupied the top floor of the four-story building, had readied it for his short stay, including stocking the fridge.

So this morning Cole had awakened in his own bed refreshed and looking out a window with a view of the Duomo, but longing for a woman an ocean away.

Give her some space, he cautioned himself. Sage had

promised to consider going out with him when he returned. It seemed ridiculous to be awaiting her answer about a date when he wanted so much more.

Surrounded by a throng of photographers with continuously clicking cameras, and security barking out orders in rapid Italian, Cole continued to make his way toward the elaborate tent where the Bertelli show was being held.

Once inside he immediately heard his name. Marie shouldered her way through the crowd. A worried expression deepened the lines in her forehead and grooves around her mouth.

"Please tell me you brought that sister of yours with you." She hissed, without preliminary, her panicked eyes searching around him.

Cole shrugged. "No. I haven't seen or talked to Lola in a few weeks," he said. "I was expecting to see her here."

"Well, she's not here. Her agency can't reach her, and she's not answering her damn phone." Marie bellowed over the din of the crowd. Forgetting her affected Italian accent, her intonation was straight out of Boston's north end. "She's supposed to wear our showstopper gown, and she's nowhere to be found."

Marie ran a hand through her short bob. "I don't know what we're going to do. I'd heard she could be unreliable at times, but I didn't think she'd screw me over, too."

Cole pulled his phone from the pocket of his suit jacket. "Hold on, I'll try giving her a call."

Three rings later, his youngest sister picked up. "Lola," Cole shouted into the phone covering his other ear with his hand.

Marie pushed aside a flap on the large tent, which led to a section that appeared to be a makeshift break room. There were pastries and bottled drinks set up on a corner table with several people milling around them.

It was a bit quieter, allowing Cole to hear what sounded like a party on the other end of the phone line.

"Hey, baby girl, where are you?" he asked, hoping both the party and his sister were nearby.

"What is she saying? Where is she?" Marie asked frantically.

Cole held up his hand as he tried to make out what his sister was saying. He only caught a few words, but they were enough to surmise what was going on.

"Met some friends…fun party…Madrid…stuck on a yacht …talk later," Lola said.

Cole called his sister's name, but either they'd been disconnected or she'd hung up. He hit the redial button. No answer.

Marie shook her head. "She's not coming at all, is she?"

"It doesn't sound like it," Cole said.

Before Marie could respond, a harried young woman carrying a clipboard approached them. From what Cole could glean from her excited, rapid-fire Italian, they'd located a last-minute replacement for Lola.

"Meno male." Marie's clasped her hands together, and her shoulders sagged in relief. She turned to Cole. "Your sister has burned a big bridge here today. If she keeps it up, no one is going to want to work with her. There aren't many girls as beautiful as she is, but there are plenty who are more reliable."

Cole loved his sister, but this time he couldn't defend her behavior. Tia had tried to talk to both him and Victor about Lola, but they'd both dismissed her concerns. Maybe it was time for them to have a sit-down with the youngest member of their family about her conduct.

An American reporter from a tabloid television show snagged Marie's attention. A camera in her face, she immediately snapped back into character with her synthetic Italian accent intact.

Cole grabbed a bottle of sparkling mineral water from the corner table. Twisting off the cap, he decided to take a few minutes before returning to the fray outside the break area.

"Ms. Bertelli, tell me, do you have any fireworks in store for us this afternoon on or off the runway?" the reporter asked.

Cole watched as Marie feigned an exaggerated disbelief at the question as she faced the cameraman. "Who, me?"

Both she and the reporter burst into conspiratorial giggles. "You'll just have to wait and see, won't you?" Marie teased.

Having had enough of watching the media dog and pony show, Cole left the break area. The crush of people had lessened considerably. With the show scheduled to start in twenty minutes, he presumed most of them had already found their seats surrounding the runway stage.

He handed an attendant his ticket and was immediately escorted down an aisle to the row of chairs closest to the stage. Sitting in his seat, Cole inclined his head at the young star of the reality show *Sugar Daddy*. The octogenarian seated on the other side of her wrapped a possessive arm around his borderline jailbait girlfriend and shot Cole a murderous look.

What in the hell had he gotten himself into?

The chair on the other side of him was vacant, and Cole didn't even want to speculate who would eventually sit in it. He glanced at his watch. Hopefully, this freak show would start on time and wrap up quickly.

"Is this seat taken?"

Cole's body recognized her voice before his brain could kick into gear, and his heart thumped wildly against his rib cage. Slowly he turned toward the familiar sound, hoping it wasn't a product of wishful thinking.

"Sage." Standing, he smiled as he said her name.

She wore a red wrap dress, his favorite color on her, and ridiculously high heels. Her coat was draped over an arm, and her kinky curls were piled on top of her head in some kind of updo his fingers itched to set free.

"I thought I imagined you," she said, the grin on her face rivaled his. "I can't believe you're here. When? How?"

Cole pulled her into his arms and stifled her questions with a kiss. He didn't care about the how or the why. He was just thrilled to see her, to hold her, to kiss her.

Sage flung her arms around his neck. She moaned softly into his mouth as his tongue caressed hers. The tenderness of the kiss belied his all-consuming hunger for her.

A few moments later, Cole ended the kiss but only so he could look at her face again and reassure himself she was really in his arms.

"I missed you." They said the words simultaneously as they took their seats.

Cole reached for Sage's hand. He didn't ever want to let it go. He didn't ever want to let her go. Again, his body instinctively knew what his brain had yet to register.

He'd fallen hard for Sage Matthews.

She squeezed his hand, and Cole gripped hers even tighter. He would have thought his feelings would have him running scared in the opposite direction. Instead, his fear was the very real possibility she didn't feel the same way.

For now, he simply wanted to revel in the fact that for this moment they were together. Cole raised Sage's hand to his lips. As he kissed it, he caught sight of Marie from the other side on the wide runway stage. Even at a distance, he could make out the frown on her face.

Realization dawned and he nearly laughed aloud. It

looked as though Bertelli's showing of the upcoming fall
and winter fashions was going to have to stand on its own
because a ceasefire had been declared in the battle between
Nashville's two cosmetics companies. From now on, he
and Sage would be making love, not war.

"Oh, my God, I think I just spotted Marie Bertelli,"
Sage said. "If I didn't know better, I'd think she was scowl-
ing at us."

"You're imagining things," Cole said, not wanting to
ruin the show for her.

Shortly afterward, the lights dimmed and music began
to play as an announcer welcomed the audience, in both
English and Italian, to the showing of the House of Bertelli's ready-to-wear collection for the fall and winter sea-
sons.

The models soon began strutting down the catwalk
dressed in sweaters, dresses and coats in the autumnal
colors of orange, yellow and rich brown. The clothes were
stunning, Cole thought. He could hear Sage's excited *oohs*
and *aahs* at nearly every piece.

Too bad Marie didn't realize she wouldn't need controversy to grab a share of the spotlight for her talented
team of designers.

A leggy model walked onto the stage wearing a short
yellow dress and a pair of high-heeled black boots. Immediately, Cole imagined those studded boots on Sage.

He leaned over and put his lips against her ear. "I want
to see you wearing those boots and red lipstick," he said.
"Nothing else."

"I suppose you want me back in that linen closet, too."
Sage spoke into his ear so only he could hear.

Cole was about to tell her exactly where he wanted her,
when a disturbance broke out in the other front row on the

opposite side of the runway. He recognized the faces instantly, a rapper-turned-actor yelling at a boxer.

Both the music playing in the background and the models onstage came to an abrupt halt.

"Stay the hell away from my wife," the irate former rapper yelled.

The boxer bellowed a string of curses in reply.

Some of the models fled the stage in their teetering heels while others turned to watch the rapidly escalating argument. Security guards were pushing toward the fracas, but not before the former rapper threw a punch that connected with the boxer's jaw.

It appeared Marie was getting too much of the controversy she'd wanted.

Cole turned to Sage. "Let's get out of here."

She nodded her agreement. With the crowds edging closer to the melee, the two of them were able to easily slip out of the giant tent.

Sage shook her head in amazement. "Who's dumb idea was it to sit them next to each other?" she asked. "Their social media beef has been all over the news."

Cole shrugged. The same person who'd thought, after that article in *America Today*, that seating them next to each other would generate tabloid headlines, he thought. However, he'd explain all that to her later. Right now, he just wanted to enjoy her company.

"Have you eaten?" He asked as they navigated the tents, equipment and people in the castle's courtyard to the street.

"Not yet," she said.

"Then you're in for a treat," he said. "Walk with me." Cole held out his arm, and she linked hers through it.

He hesitated, glancing down at her shoes. "Can you handle a fifteen-minute walk in those?"

"I'll do my best," she said. "I've never seen more fashionably dressed people in my life than I've seen here. Not even in Paris."

Cole nodded as they walked along the narrow walkways leading to their destination. "What Milan lacks in Roman monuments and Renaissance splendor, it makes up for on the fashion front."

A long line snaking down the street signaled to him that they'd made it to their destination. Sage frowned as they stood at the end of it. "I have no idea what we're waiting for, but are you sure it's worth it?"

"Absolutely." Cole patted her arm, still looped through his "You will, too, once you taste a *panzerotti* from Luini's. It's a Milan institution."

Fortunately, the long line gave them a chance to talk, and Cole filled Sage in on the reason he suspected Marie Bertelli had personally invited them to her fashion show.

Sage snuggled into him. "I should probably be offended, but right now I couldn't care less why we're here. I'm just glad we're together."

Cole disentangled his arm from hers, and then wrapped both his arms around her waist. The heart this woman had managed to capture in such a short time expanded in his chest as he kissed the top of her head.

Finally, they made it through the doors of Luini's and were soon walking out again, their hands wrapped around the bakery's specialty.

Sage peeled the paper wrapper back on the half moon–shaped pocket of fried dough as they stood outside the bakery. Hers was stuffed with cheese and tomato sauce. "They look like fancy Hot Pockets." She inhaled. "But it smells heavenly."

"Try it," Cole encouraged.

He watched her take a tentative bite. A smile formed on her face as she chewed. "Oh, my God, the dough is sweet.

This is like having your meal and dessert in one." Immediately, she took another bite.

"So was it worth waiting in line?"

"I'd wait in a line ten times as long for one of these," she said enthusiastically.

Cole had pulled back the wrapper on his salami-and-mozzarella-stuffed panzerotti and was poised to dig in to it when a familiar figure approached.

The man slapped Cole on the back, a broad smile on his face. "So it is you," he said. "I thought I saw you at the Bertelli show earlier before that fight broke out. So when did you get to town, Admiral?"

"Oh, now that you're not working for me, you can call me that to my face." Cole laughed at Sean Cox, the man he'd hired to work at Force Cosmetics when was a kid fresh out of college.

Years later, when Cole left Force, he'd recommended the young man as his replacement.

Sean laughed. "Back then I was too busy quaking in my boots to even think it."

Cole remembered his manners. "Sean Cox, this is…"

"Sage Matthews of Stiletto Cosmetics," Sean finished, turning to Sage. "I've read about you and your company."

As the two shook hands, a mental red flag went up in Cole's head. More like his former protégé had been briefed on Sage's company.

Sean gave Cole a pointed look. "In fact, I was on a conference call the other day where *both of your companies* were mentioned."

Cole nodded, getting Sean's message loud and clear. Force Cosmetics wanted to add both Espresso and Stiletto to their brand portfolio. The only question was what lengths would the mammoth company go to in order to acquire them?

They talked a few more minutes and then Sean excused himself so he could stand in the growing line for his own panzerotti. "I'll be in touch," Sean said to Cole, as they parted.

Cole turned his attention back to Sage. He decided not to mention the impending offers for their companies that were almost sure to come from Force. Not yet. At this point, it was speculation on his part. Besides, there would be plenty of time for them to obsess over work.

For now, he wanted to continue to enjoy this time with her.

"So are you free for the rest of the afternoon?" Cole took a bite of his forgotten panzerotti.

"My schedule just happens to be clear for the next two days," Sage said.

"So what would like to do?" Cole asked. "We could take a walk along the rooftop of the Duomo or go shopping along the Quadrilatero d'Oro. Just say the word, and I'll take you anywhere you want to go."

She smiled up at him. Her brown eyes held their mischievous spark. "Take me to bed."

Chapter 15

Patience wasn't Sage's strong suit.

"Delayed gratification is for saints and suckers," she said, when they arrived at her hotel room. "I'm neither."

Housekeeping had turned down the bed, which beckoned a few feet from where they stood. Foil-wrapped chocolates adorned the plump pillows. However, there was only one sweet confection Sage was interested in unwrapping, and it was rock hard and pressed against her belly.

Sage ground against him as he held her. Cole's sharp intake of breath indicated she was one step closer to getting the satisfaction they both wanted.

"You're killing me," Cole whispered.

"Good," Sage said, continuing the slow grind. "Think of it as payback."

"Payback? After spending last weekend together, I assumed we were both out of the retaliation business."

Sage slid her index finger down the soft cashmere of

his sweater to the center of his chest. "That was before my sleepless journey across the Atlantic, where all I did was yearn for your touch, ache for your kiss and dream of having you naked and inside me."

Cole gulped. Sage watched his Adam's apple bob in his throat as he struggled with his resolve. He dropped his arms from around her waist, and then took a step back.

"It's obvious I want you." He glanced down at the bulge in his pants. *"Badly."*

Sage raised a brow and inclined her head toward the bed.

Shaking his head, Cole grasped her hands. "But I don't want a romp on a hotel bed." He raised her hands to his lips and pressed a kiss to them. "Not with you."

The intensity of Cole's gaze startled her. His dark brown eyes brimmed with an emotion Sage had never seen in them before. Or perhaps it was a reflection of her own feelings and the emotion she'd been waylaid by this afternoon at the unexpected sight of him—*love*.

Sage froze, startled by the realization. It didn't make sense. They were competitors. It was too soon, she told herself, but her heart wasn't buying into it.

"I want to take you to my place," Cole continued. "To my bed, where I plan to take my time making love to every inch of you until we're both too exhausted to move."

Sage's legs wobbled slightly at the illicit images his words brought to mind. "I promise to make it worth the wait." His melodic baritone rumbled through her.

Pull yourself together, she silently admonished, struggling to maintain her outer cool. Her insides, like her panties, were already on meltdown.

"Okay, you've convinced me," Sage said, managing to keep her voice from quivering like the rest of her body. She eyed his erection, which appeared on the verge of breaking through the front of his pants. "As long as I get what I want."

Cole followed her gaze. "Oh, you'll get it all right."

The short time it took them to check out of her hotel and arrive at Cole's place felt like an eternity to Sage. She'd clung to his hand during the short walk, savoring the innocuous contact of his skin on hers as he made lazy circles against her palm. She'd barely registered walking hurriedly along the unremarkable streets of the metropolitan city center, past the famed Duomo and ducking down narrow cobblestone side streets to avoid the chaotic temporary fashion hub set up around the Sforzesco Castle.

There was only one attraction Sage was interested in right now, and although it wasn't in her guidebook, she was positive it was the best this city would have to offer her this afternoon.

Cole stuck his key in the door of a charming older building that age and decades of summers had bleached into a muted shade of gold. Red shutters and window boxes surrounded its windows. Inside, he cast a glance at the ancient elevator, which, like the building, appeared to be a nineteenth-century throwback.

"I'm on the fourth floor, but you can't always trust the elevator," he said, then looked at her shoes. "I'll carry you if you'd like."

Sage eyed the steep flight of stairs. "I'll walk now, but save your energy." She shot him a look she hoped conveyed her meaning. "I anticipate climbing aboard and riding later."

Before she could register what was happening, Cole scooped her up in one swift motion. The air came out of her lungs with a whoosh as he tossed her over his shoulder caveman-style.

"Then it's *your* energy we'd better conserve," he said. "It's going to be a wild ride."

"That's mighty big talk," Sage called out from over his shoulder. "Hope you can…"

A sudden smack on her ass silenced her.

"Save that brash, sassy mouth of yours for when I get you upstairs," Cole said.

Sage pressed her lips together and did as he ordered. The general was fully prepared to let the admiral take charge.

With one hand lifting her suitcase and the other holding her firmly by the backside, Cole effortlessly climbed the flights of stairs. He set her suitcase down long enough to unlock the door, before carrying her and it inside and kicking the door closed with his foot.

Sage lifted her head off his back and glanced around at her surroundings. The gleam of the hardwood floors, the beauty of the art on the walls and the sumptuous furnishings were lost on her. Sage didn't care where they were, as long as she was with him.

"I think you can put me down now," she said, finally.

Ignoring her suggestion, Cole marched through the living and dining rooms with her still draped over his shoulder and his hand still splayed on her backside. As his sure stride ate up a long corridor off the dining room, Sage couldn't help noticing that, while he'd said his condo was on the fourth floor of the building, he'd failed to mention it was the entire fourth floor.

Sage felt her excitement build with every step he took. The brief tour ended in a bedroom large enough to fit her entire house into with room to spare.

Windows took up one wall, and although the draperies were drawn Sage was sure they offered a spectacular view of the city. She raised her head to see a sitting area on one side of the huge bedroom, with a large flat-screen television, sofa and plush armchairs. However, it was the half of the room behind her, which she'd caught a glimpse of as he carried her inside, that Sage found most appealing.

A king-size bed dominated it, rich mahogany wood as masculine as the man who slept in it. Sage's breath caught in her throat at a vision of their nude bodies transforming the pristine silver-gray bedding into a tangled mess of sweaty sheets.

Cole's hands moved to her waist and lifted her from his shoulders. He held her close enough for her body to slowly slide down the length of his until they were standing toe-to-toe.

Their gazes connected, and again his eyes radiated more than lust. He brushed a kiss across her mouth.

"Turn around," he said. "I want to show you something."

Sage faced the bed. Cole wrapped his arms around her and nuzzled her neck. His thick, impossibly hard erection pressed against her buttocks, and she bit her bottom lip to suppress a shiver.

"You're not the only one who couldn't sleep a wink last night." He whispered near her ear. "I lay awake in that very bed reliving all the things we did this past weekend. Then I fantasized about what I'd do to you and then beg you to do to me when I saw you again."

Staring at the bed, Sage released a shaky breath and licked her suddenly dry lips. "You should know by now that you don't have to beg." She turned in his embrace and raised her chin until her eyes met his. "Just tell me your fantasy."

Then an even better idea occurred to her. She grasped the collar of his jacket and slid it down over his broad shoulders until it fell off him onto the floor. Shredding her own coat, she tossed it on top of his. "On second thought, don't tell me. Let me guess."

"Guess?" Cole asked, his expression a mix of confusion and intrigue.

Sage nodded. Touching her palm to the center of his chest, she walked him backward to one of the armchairs across the room.

"I'm going to guess what you wanted to do to me last night and every little thing you wanted me to do to you." She pushed against his chest until he dropped into the chair, and then she leaned in until the tips of their noses met. "You tell me if I'm hot or cold."

"I can tell you now, you're hot as hell." Cole traced her bottom lip with his tongue, but she pulled back before she instinctively opened her mouth to him.

"Uh-uh." Sage wagged an admonishing finger. "Get comfortable, Mr. Sinclair, because this game is just getting started."

He eased back in the armchair. His dark eyes were glued to her every move as she slowly backed away. She made the mistake of stealing a glance at his crotch, and his cock twitched in response as if she'd called it by name.

Sage's mouth went dry and her panties dampened. The sight of it straining against his pants, hard and ready, nearly made her forget about the sexy game.

She closed her eyes to temporarily block it from her mind. Later, she intended to give it the attention it deserved. Sage dropped her chin to her chest, and raised her arms to her head to remove the bobby pins anchoring her updo. Relaxing her neck, she shook her head and fluffed her coils back into full-on Afro status.

Sage opened her eyes and looked at him sitting in the chair. "Fantasy-wise, am I hot or cold?"

"Hot," Cole said. "How did you know the first thing I

wanted to do when I saw you at the fashion show was set that wild hair free?"

"Because it's like we're two of a kind." Sage skimmed her hands downward over her breasts and the sensitive peaks of her nipples to the sash of her wrap dress at her waist. "And despite what some may view as a short acquaintance, we know each other almost as well as we know ourselves."

She yanked at the sash, and her dress fell open, revealing the lacy bra and matching panties underneath. Both were a soft shade of cotton-candy pink.

Sage shrugged off the dress, and let it drop to the floor. Clad in only her underwear and her heels, she posed the same question. "Am I hot or cold?"

"Damn, girl." Cole's reply was more of a groan, and his hands gripped the sides of the armchair.

Sage smiled, reveling in her feminine power, the game turning her on as much as it did him. "Sorry, but that's not one of the options," she said. "Again, hot or cold?"

"Hot." Cole shifted in the chair. Sage guessed it was to accommodate his growing cock, which looked as though it would break right through his zipper. "But I have to confess, those sweet and innocent pink undies aren't what I expected to see on a woman so deliciously naughty."

Sage pivoted to provide him with a backside view of her barely-there thong. She heard his sharp intake of breath as she looked back at him over her shoulder. "I assure you, I'm naughty to the bone."

"I wouldn't have it any other way," Cole said, his eyes riveted to her bare ass cheeks. "So far, you're my fantasy come to life."

Next, Sage moved to kick off one of her high heel pumps.

"Whoa. Cold," his deep voice called out without being prompted. "*Brrr!* Ice-cold."

She turned her head and smiled at him as she undid the front clasp on her bra. She let the straps slip from her shoulders, before letting it fall to the floor.

"Maybe this will help thaw the chill." Sage slowly spun around, now naked except for her heels and panties. There was no need for her to ask the question that had ruled their game. Cole's eyes darkened. She could feel the fire in his hungry gaze as it traveled from her breasts down to her heels and back up again.

"Very, very hot." He patted his lap. "Now, bring it here."

Gooseflesh erupted on Sage's skin at the husky command. Every cell in her body wanted to obey, but she steeled herself against the overwhelming urge. Instead, she allowed her eyes the pleasure of roaming from his strong jaw, covered in a shadow of beard she could hardly wait to feel against her mouth and between her thighs, to his broad chest and then downward to the tented slacks he'd had on entirely too long.

"Your turn," she said. "Take off your clothes."

Sage watched the corner of his mouth quirk upward into a lazy half smile. "Is that an order, General?"

"Please." Her dulcet tone belied the fact she was seconds away from marching over to that chair and tearing the clothes off him.

His grin widened. "Well, since you asked so nicely."

Standing, Cole grabbed the bottom of his sweater, and pulled it up and over his head. Sage sank her teeth into her bottom lip to suppress a gasp. Her fingertips tingled in anticipation of touching his solid wall of a chest, then clinging to those broad shoulders. She could hardly wait to feel those strong arms surround her within the confines of his embrace.

Sage looked on, mesmerized as Cole eased his zipper over his erection. Pants and underwear hit the floor, and his cock sprang free. Every bit as long, thick and hard as she remembered and, *oh*, the things he could do with it.

She opened her mouth to speak as he kicked away his shoes and socks, but her mind went blank. The gift for the snappy comeback eluded her. So did the ability of speech. All she could do was stare, stammer and drool.

Cole didn't miss her reaction. "You speechless?"

Sage assumed he raised a brow, but she wasn't looking at his face. Her nipples tightened, and her minuscule thong panties barely contained the moisture pooling between her legs.

He sat back in the chair and stroked his length once, then again. "Come, ride me," he said. Then he added in that rich melodic baritone that never failed to send shivers down her spine. *"Pretty please."*

"Well, since you asked so nicely." Her speech restored, Sage echoed his words of just minutes before as she did a slow strut toward the armchair.

She stopped short. "Condom?"

"My wallet." Cole inclined his head at his pants, which were currently beneath the spike heel of her shoe.

Sage retrieved the foil packet, then flung both his wallet and pants aside. She leaned over the chair and brushed aside the hand gripping the base of his cock, replacing it with hers.

"I'll take it from here." She allowed herself to stroke the magnificent length of the shaft, from base to the smooth, velvet tip.

"Don't." Cole gasped loudly. "Do that again and this will be over before it even starts."

Cole pulled her onto the chair, and Sage straddled him, her heated core hovering inches above his hardness.

He threaded his fingers through her hair. Fisting a clump of the tight coils in his hand, he crushed his mouth to hers. Sage moaned, and he plunged his tongue inside her mouth, deepening the kiss. The taste of him, his cologne, a heady mix of spice tinged with rum, nearly driving her out of her mind.

Close to getting what she'd been craving ever since their weekend together had ended, Sage ripped open the condom wrapper. She wrenched her mouth away from his and quickly sheathed him.

"I have never wanted anyone as much as I want you," she said.

Their gazes connected. "You own me, Sage Matthews, heart, body and soul." Even in the heat of passion, his words rang with sincerity, and Sage knew without a doubt, this man loved her as much as she loved him. "Now come get what's yours."

Sage moved to slip her thong panties aside, but he released her hair and clutched the scant fabric in his hand. She heard the lace rip as he tore them from her body and tossed them to the floor.

His forcefulness sent an erotic thrill coursing through her, and Sage couldn't wait any longer. Slowly, she lowered herself onto his cock inch by delectable inch.

Their simultaneous moans echoed throughout the room as he stretched and filled her. A rush of sensations bombarded her core, and her walls contracted around him. The overwhelming power of their connection, both physical and emotional, took her by surprise.

"Ah," Cole rasped. His body froze, and he touched his forehead to hers, as if he, too, needed a moment to regain control. "You're so tight. And so damn hot."

Sage rose and slid down his steely length. Then she did it again and again. The next time, Cole thrust upward to meet her in one stroke, followed by another and another easing her into a slow, steady ride.

He trailed kisses from her throat to her breasts, which he cupped in his large hands. She groaned when his thumbs brushed over the sensitive peaks. The feel of his hands, of him inside her, threatened to send her over the edge.

He flicked his tongue over a nipple and then covered it with his mouth.

"Cole." Sage threw her head back and called his name as he alternated sucking and teasing. Moving from one breast to the other, the man's tongue, lips and teeth were as relentless as the upward thrusts that continued to fill her over and over.

She called his name again, and he raised his head, capturing her lips in a kiss. He swallowed her moan of delight as his tongue delved into her mouth.

Driven by excitement and ravenous need, Sage's thighs squeezed against his and her slick walls clamped around him. Her body acted of its own accord. She could barely handle what he dished out, yet everything in her begged for more.

Cole's hands slid from her breasts over her belly button down to her hips. His fingers gripped her roughly, breaking both their kiss and the rhythm of their ride.

"You feel so good. I want to make this last forever." He stilled, his tone both harsh and pleading.

Catching her breath, Sage stared into the depths of his eyes. "You own me, Cole Sinclair, heart, body and soul," she whispered, her voice cracked with emotion. "Now take what's yours, because it only gets better."

Cole's fingers dug into her hips. His gaze didn't waver as he surged upward. Sage gasped at the force of the powerful thrust and the ones that followed it. Her hands moved from his chest to his broad shoulders, and she held on tight.

Rising and falling on his cock, she met each of his deep strokes. Harder and faster. The more he gave her, the more she craved until spasms of pure pleasure ripped through her. Wave after wave, the orgasm overpowered her very being.

With one last violent stroke, Cole yelled her name. He followed her over the edge, his hands clutching her hips as his cock pulsated inside her.

She sagged against him, and he encircled her in his embrace. As their hearts slammed against their chests, Sage wasn't surprised to feel them throb to the exact same beat.

Then the words weighing on her heart unintentionally escaped her lips. *"I love you."*

Chapter 16

"Do you always hold a Q&A session after sex?"

If Sage thought her question would dissuade him, she was mistaken, Cole thought. "It's a simple question," he said. "I even made it multiple choice so it would be easy for you to answer."

The woman cradled in his arms sighed contentedly and snuggled deeper into his chest. Their marathon had come full circle, starting in the armchair, moving on to his bed, next beneath the shower spray and now finally back to the chair again.

Cole adjusted the flannel throw he'd yanked off the sofa over their naked bodies. He'd finally relented and let her take off those sexy shoes. Now her bare feet were tucked under her as she leaned against him.

"Well?" he persisted.

"Could you repeat the question?" Sage hedged.

He shifted in the chair until they were face-to-face.

"When you said you loved me earlier, did you mean it, or did I put it on you so good, I had you talking out of your head?"

Sage snorted. "Nothing wrong with your ego."

Her tone was filled with the playful banter that had become a hallmark of their relationship. Yet, the straight-forward woman who never backed down from him, or anyone else, averted her eyes. The drapes were open, and she stared out the window, which offered a picturesque view of the starlit night sky and the city in the distance.

Cole let his question sink in. Despite her facade of bravado, she was scared. Her hesitance wasn't in deciding on an answer, but rather whether to trust him with it.

Pushing Sage probably wasn't his best idea. Yet, he needed to hear it. He needed to know if she was as caught up in the whirlwind of a romance that could be as challenging and infuriating as it was heartfelt and sexy. The more layers he pulled back from the complicated, smart and beautiful woman in his arms, the more he found to admire, respect and, yes, love.

Everything in the way she'd responded as he made love to her told him she felt the exact same way. However, he had to know for sure.

Cole smoothed his knuckles down the side of her cheek. She sighed softly as she met finally met his gaze. Her body trembled against him.

"I probably shouldn't feed that massive ego of yours." She tapped her forefinger against his bare chest. "But I can't deny the fact that you indeed put it on me, and that thing you did with your tongue in the shower made me forget my own name."

Though he should probably be flattered, Cole felt his hopes deflate. It hadn't been the answer he'd wanted or expected. He kept his expression impassive to hide his disappointment as she continued.

"I also can't deny the fact that I love you," she said. "I meant everything I told you when we made love."

Cole exhaled, his disappointment replaced by pure delight. He knew he was grinning like an idiot, but he didn't care. "Now was that so hard to say?"

"No, but it does make things complicated."

"It doesn't have to be," he said. "I love you. You love me. I can't think of anything simpler."

Sage rested her head on his chest. "Right here. Right now, that's true. But eventually we have to get back to the real world. Our real lives. Loving you doesn't change the fact that we're competitors, or that you want my company."

Cole did want Stiletto Cosmetics. However, real life had indeed intruded, and now he wanted Sage more. Enough to find an alternative solution to solving Espresso's problems.

She craned her neck to look up at him. "I'm sorry. I shouldn't have brought up work," she said. "As important as Stiletto is to me, I'm enjoying this time with you too much to think about it right now."

He dropped a kiss on her forehead. "But since you did bring it up, I think we need to talk about it. Returning to Nashville and our real lives is only a problem if we make it one."

Sage sighed. "That sounds good when we're together and naked, but eventually we'll have to put our clothes on and go to work."

"I'm rescinding my offer to buy Stiletto," Cole said. He didn't add that he had a strong suspicion she'd soon get one from Force Cosmetics. At this point, it was still speculation and would further complicate a situation he was trying to make easier for both of them.

Sage sat up and looked at him. A surprised expression blanketed her pretty features.

"There are other ways to put the brakes on Espresso's downhill slide, ones that don't include acquiring your company," he said.

Sage continued to stare at him. "I don't understand," she began. Then a corner of her mouth quirked up into a half smile. "Or did I put it on you so good, it made your forget about coming after my company."

"Touché." Cole threw his head back and laughed. "But to be honest, I think I actually made the decision to back off when we were at my aunt's house for dinner."

"I don't get it. Did your aunt say something to change your mind? Or was that what you and Riley were talking about when I was out of earshot?"

"No, on both counts," he said, his tone growing serious. "It was what you said about your mother." Cole's shrug belied how much that part of the dinner conversation had gotten under his skin. "Before Victor and then my younger sisters came along, my mother was also a single parent. My father died in a construction accident a few months after I was born, so I have no memory of him. However, I do remember the struggle and the sacrifices my mom made to start Espresso."

It wasn't something Cole talked about often, if ever, especially after the last angry conversation he'd had with his mother. He'd been young, brash and stupid. If he'd only known it was to be their last conversation, he would have handled things so differently.

Unfortunately, there was no way to turn back the hands of time, or for the older and wiser man he was now to shake some sense into the hotheaded kid he'd been then.

Sage rested her head back on his chest, and he smoothed

a hand through her hair, which felt like soft puffs of cotton beneath his fingertips.

"I guess I always thought of you as coming from money, and then being savvy enough to make more of it," she said. "I didn't see the struggle."

"Mom took the insurance check she got after my father died to start Espresso, so I grew up with it, just me and her. In fact, my earliest memories are of stuffing lipstick and compacts into boxes to help her fill mail orders. I felt like it was our business."

It was why one of his mother's last decisions had cut him to the core. The dull pang he carried around like a piece of luggage surfaced in his chest.

Again, she lifted her head and faced him. "Then why did you leave Espresso to work for Force?" She asked. "I wondered about it when you mentioned it during that first lunch downtown. Listening to you now has made me even more curious. You and your mom started a cosmetics empire, what on earth would make you walk away from it?"

Ordinarily, Cole would shut down at this point. Find a way to change the subject or ignore the question altogether. While Sage probably wouldn't press him for an answer, he found himself wanting to share things with her he didn't tell anyone else. He wanted her to know it all, the good, the bad, even the ugly.

"It's a long story, and some of it's not very pretty," he said finally.

She squirmed against him in the chair and readjusted the throw. "I'm a captive audience," she said. "Besides, the fact we're similar in so many ways means I already know so much about you. I want to hear all the things I don't know."

Exhaling, Cole began to explain, starting with the good. "My mom was a lot like us—confident, hardworking, competitive and stubborn as hell." He smoothed Sage's hair off her face and dropped a kiss on her forehead. "As a young widow with an infant, she received a lot of advice from well-meaning people who thought she should find a part-time job, put the insurance check from my father's death in the bank and live off the profits from the construction company my father owned with his brother."

"Riley's dad?" Sage asked.

"Yes. My late uncle Simon," Cole said. "He also built the Espresso building. Anyway, my mom obviously didn't follow their advice. She sold my father's interest in Sinclair Construction to my uncle, and she used the money from it, along with the insurance check, to start Espresso."

Sage craned her neck to look up at him. "Gutsy move. Especially nearly thirty-five years ago when it was more difficult being a woman in business."

"Mom said she did it for me. Because I'd lost a father I wouldn't remember having. She wanted to give me more than just a decent childhood. She wanted to give me a legacy, something that could be passed down from generation to generation."

The woman in his arms was quiet. She placed her hand over his, and Cole could feel the warmth and understanding in her touch.

"She worked hard for it, and she pushed me hard, too. Mom never let up on me, even after she married Victor and my sisters were born. She was constantly grooming me to one day take over Espresso," Cole said. "I followed her blueprint, working at Espresso part-time through high school and college and, of course, every summer. After graduation, I became one of the company's two vice presidents, my stepfather was the other one."

"Was that a problem for you?" Sage asked.

"Not initially," Cole said. "We were responsible for different departments, but we both reported to my mother, who always had the final word. The three of us worked well together. Besides, Victor's been in my life since I was eight. He's the one who helped me with my homework as a kid and showed up at my Little League games, even more often than my mom."

"What changed the dynamic?" Sage asked.

Sharing the good had been easier than Cole had expected. He'd genuinely enjoyed working with his parents. Even after he'd bought his town house, he frequently ate dinner at their house where, in spite of Tia and Lola's protests, they often talked business.

"New companies came on the scene. They began offering women of color, our core customers, new product lines and trendier colors. Also, mainstream brands like Force began to step up their game in catering to the growing multiethinic market," Cole explained. "Every time I brought it up with Mom or Victor, along with ideas to keep Espresso competitive, they shut me down. My mom didn't take it or me seriously. She believed those companies were flashes in the pan that wouldn't last long and that the best course of action for Espresso was to continue what we were doing. Do what we do and do it well, she'd say."

Cole summed up the two years he'd spent warning his parents the business was rapidly changing and imploring with them to make changes. Each time they'd rejected his suggestions and dismissed his concerns. "The more I tried to talk to them about it, the more my mom dug her heels in."

"Stubborn." They said the word simultaneously, knowing the same could be said of them.

"Then she got sick and, despite the treatments, we all knew she wouldn't get better." Cole told her in as few words as possible about his mother's breast cancer battle and felt Sage hold his hand a bit tighter.

It reinforced his decision to confide in her. Cole exhaled a shaky breath. "When she was advised to get her affairs in order, she met with her lawyers at her bedside."

Time hadn't faded the smell of prolonged sickness and impending death that came back to him when he thought about his mother's final days. It was then that the memory of the cancer-ravaged version of her overshadowed the vibrant, demanding, beautiful force to be reckoned with that Selina Sinclair Gray had been the majority of her life.

"Afterward she informed me Victor was the new president of Espresso. She said my ideas were too radical, and at twenty-six, I was simply too young to leave in charge of the company I'd always believed we'd built together."

Sage kept a firm grip on his hand. He wasn't proud of how he'd reacted to his mother's decision. Unfortunately, life didn't offer do overs.

"We were both hotheads. I said some harsh things out of anger. So did she," he said. "She told me to get out of her sight, to which I replied, 'Gladly, I don't want to look at you right now, either.'"

Cole sighed. He'd never before shared his last conversation with his mother with anyone. The most he'd said to his family was that they'd had words.

"I had driven halfway back to my place—then I turned the car around to go back and apologize, but it was too late. She was dead."

The toughest part of the story already told, Cole pushed through to the end. "After she died, Victor and I continued to butt heads at work over the same issues. Only he was even more resistant to making changes and had the final say," he said. "I didn't want to continue arguing with the only parent I had left, so I handed in my resignation and left both Espresso and Nashville. A few months later, I went to work at Force."

Cole was relieved when Sage didn't offer up meaningless platitudes, which only tended to make the person saying them feel better. Nor did she try telling him that despite their horrible argument, his mother loved him. He already knew she did.

Instead, Sage released his hand and then she wrapped her arms around his neck and hugged him tighter than he'd ever been hugged in his life.

"It's why you try to think first instead of acting out of anger, isn't it?" she asked.

Cole nodded. "It was a lesson I learned the hard way," he said. "If I could do it all again, instead of lashing out I would have simply told my mother how much her decision hurt. I'd ask her why, after years of making Espresso my number one priority, she didn't have enough faith in me to know I would do whatever was best for our company. The bottom line is, in the end, she didn't trust me."

"Yet, you're back at Espresso now, trying to stage its comeback," Sage said.

Cole nodded. Despite, his bank balance and business experience, he still was a man with something to prove, if only to himself. "That angry exchange with my mother is a weight I'll carry with me forever," he said. "But knowing I put the company she poured her entire life into back on top will help ease the burden."

Tears brimmed in Sage's eyes when she met his gaze. "The woman in me who loves you wants to do everything in her power to help you achieve that goal." Her voice cracked with emotion. "But to my business side, we're still competitors."

Cole swiped away one of the tears with the pad of his thumb before it could roll down her cheek.

"I didn't tell you all this to further complicate things between us. But when you told us about your mother at dinner, it helped me understand why Stiletto is more than a company to you," he said. "The more important you became to me, the more I needed you to know why I have to save Espresso."

"I do understand." She snuggled back into him. "I also think Nashville just might be big enough for two cosmetic companies."

Cole shifted in the chair, so he could see her face. "Does this mean our temporary cease-fire is permanent?"

"I'm ready to wave the white flag if you agree." She laughed.

"Agreed." Cole extended his hand, and she shook it.

Sage resumed her position, resting her head on his chest. "Great. Now that we've brokered the peace, I can finally stop worrying what you have up your sleeve and get a good night's sleep."

"Oh, you'll have a good night." He caressed her bare bottom with his hand. "But I doubt you'll get much sleep."

Sage rose, hands clapping enthusiastically with the rest of the audience as the cast of *Aida* took their final bows to thunderous applause.

The house lights came up, and the throng of opera patrons slowly began to exit the lavish auditorium of the Teatro alla Scala opera house. Exuberant conversations in several languages broke out all around her. She didn't have to understand what they were saying to know they were all buzzing about the performance they'd obviously enjoyed as much as she had.

"I'm not sure what was more beautiful, those powerful voices or this place." Sage soaked in the gilded wood and red velvet interior of the world-renowned venue.

She felt Cole's hand at the small of her back as they walked through the majestic mirror-lined foyer and out into the night. Even through the layers of her coat and dress, the gesture sent a warm shiver down her spine. Moreover, it made a woman who'd always taken care of herself feel protected, cherished and very much loved.

"Neither. You are the most beautiful thing about this entire evening," Cole said.

Sage snorted to hide her delight at the compliment. "You don't have to sweet-talk me," she said. "You're definitely getting lucky tonight."

"Already?" Cole joked. "Technically this is only our first date."

Sage linked her arm through his as they continued the short walk back to his place. "When it comes to you, I'm easy."

"And I meant what I said—you look stunning tonight. When I saw you in that dress, my eyes nearly popped out of my head."

"I'm glad you like it."

After taking in a view of the city from the rooftop of the Duomo cathedral and viewing Leonardo da Vinci's masterpiece *The Last Supper* at the Santa Maria delle Grazie church that morning, they'd spent the afternoon in the upscale shopping area know as the Quadrilatero d'Oro, home to the country's top designer logos.

"There nothing I love more than seeing you in a sexy red dress," Cole said. "What I didn't like was your adamantly refusing to let me buy it for you."

Sage grunted in response. Just as she had when he'd attempted to pull out his credit card at the counter of the chic designer store.

"I can pay for my own clothes." The dress had indeed been pricey, but it had been her one and only splurge.

"That's not the point."

The wide city streets narrowed into side streets as they got closer to Cole's condo. Sage's heels clicked against the cobblestones. They'd already discussed it, and she refused to rise to his bait.

"You wouldn't let me buy you anything," He continued to rant. "Not the other dresses or the shoes and boots you were practically drooling over. I could see in your eyes that you wanted all of them."

"It's called window shopping, Cole," Sage said, patiently.

"What good is having money if you can't spend it on the people you care about?" he countered.

Sage halted midstep, a few feet from the entrance to his building. She extricated her arm from his. He stopped walking and faced her. Their gazes locked. "I don't want anything from you…but you," she said.

Cole pushed out a defeated sigh. "Stubborn."

"Right back at ya." Sage looped her arm back through his, and they resumed walking.

"Life with you is never going to be easy, is it?" Humor permeated his deep voice.

"Nothing worth having ever is."

Later that night, after they'd given both Cole's bed and their favorite chair a long, hard workout, Sage stood at the window wearing one of his T-shirts, staring out at the city. She'd arrived here excited to attend her first international runway show. Now it was a forgettable footnote.

She felt Cole's arms encircle her as he came up from behind. The shadow of beard clinging to his jaw tickled her neck as he bestowed it with a series of kisses.

"I was thinking we could spend the next few days at Lake Como," he said. "I sold my villa there when I left my job at Force, but we can stay…"

Sage stopped him. "I leave for home tomorrow evening."

"Can't your staff hold down the fort at Stiletto for another day or two?"

She shook her head. "It's not work. I have a previous engagement."

Cole raised a brow. "Then cancel or reschedule it."

"I can't," she said. "It's with another man."

Chapter 17

"You might have mentioned earlier that this other man of yours was six years old."

Cole looked on as Sage wrapped an old-fashioned candy dispenser reminiscent of a grocery-store gumball machine in festive birthday paper.

"Then I might not have had the pleasure of your company on the trip back to Nashville," she said.

When Sage said she had a previous engagement with another man back in Milan, Cole had done two things. First, he'd taken her back to bed and made love to her until the only man's name falling from her lips was his, over and over again. Next he'd booked the seats next to hers on her flights to Nashville.

They'd arrived late yesterday evening and spent the night at his town house sleeping off jet lag. This morning, they'd celebrated their return to the dirty South with breakfast at the Waffle House, and now they were at Sage's house, preparing to head to her neighbor's birthday party.

Cole slapped a red bow on top of the toy truck he'd wrapped for her. "You know, that lipstick you're wearing today suits you perfectly." He'd recognized it the moment she'd smoothed the bold red shade over her lips. "You are a badass."

She topped the wrapped candy dispenser with a huge blue bow and then rounded her kitchen table to plant a lingering kiss on his mouth. "I warned you back in Milan— I'm naughty to the bone."

At the word *bone*, Cole leaned over and whispered an equally naughty joke in her ear.

Pursing her lips into a prudish frown, Sage smacked at the arm he'd wrapped around her waist. Cole caught the mischievous spark in her eyes, just before she winked. "Later." She laughed. "We've got a party to attend."

A short while later, Cole came face-to-face with Sage's other man. Wearing a red sweatshirt emblazoned with the words *It's My Birthday*, the little boy dashed toward them the moment he spotted Sage at his front door.

"Whatcha bring me?" He blurted out in lieu of a greeting.

"Kenny!" A harried redhead admonished the kid. "Manners!"

"Whatcha bring me, *please*?" The kid added a snaggletoothed grin to his second attempt, and Cole stifled a laugh.

Shaking her head at the little boy, the woman ushered them inside her house, and Sage quickly introduced them.

"Nice to meet you, Mr. Sinclair." Evie put a restraining arm around her kid to keep him from snatching the gifts from their hands. "And this etiquette-school dropout is my son, Kenny."

"Cole," he corrected. Then he addressed the woman's son. "Happy Birthday, Kenny."

"Well, Cole, like I told Sage earlier when she said you didn't mind lending us a hand, it's much appreciated. I've got two-dozen kindergarteners and ten pizzas descending on this house in two hours and definitely need reinforcements."

"Glad to help out," Cole replied, genuinely meaning it. If being here was important to Sage. It was important to him, too.

Taking their coats and hanging them in a closet near the front door, the woman turned to look at Sage. "Thanks, again. Not many friends would leave one of the most glamorous cities in one of the most glamorous countries in the world to help out with a kiddie party."

Cole silently agreed. He wished they could have stayed longer and enjoyed some time together at Lake Como; however, Sage's loyalty to her friend impressed him. Every day he was with her, Cole found something else to love and admire about this woman.

"There was no way I was going to miss Kenny's sixth birthday," Sage said.

On cue, the birthday boy stood on tiptoe and attempted to put his ear against the wrapped box in Sage's arms. His eyes were pleading when he stared up at her. "Is there a puppy in here?"

Evie put her fists on her hips and narrowed her eyes at Sage. "There had better not be."

"Not this time," Sage said. "But it's something I think you'll like almost as much."

Kenny looked to his mother. "Can't I open just this one before the party?" he asked, quickly adding an exaggerated *please*.

"Yeah, *please*." Sage mimicked her small friend.

Evie sighed. "Oh, all right."

As she led them through to the living and dining rooms,

Cole noticed the house was laid out exactly like Sage's. It had a lived-in look about it, which, despite being a stranger, made him feel welcome.

The furniture had been pushed into corners. Three folding banquet tables covered with red paper tablecloths and surrounded by chairs occupied the dining room. The living room was filled with children's games.

Sage placed her present on one of the tables then hoisted Kenny until he was standing on one of the chairs. "Happy Birthday," she said.

Without preliminaries, Kenny ripped the wrapping paper off the box as the adults stood by and watched.

"Hey! It's a candy machine," he yelled excitedly, "full of Skittles!"

Kenny threw his arms around Sage and hugged her. "Thanks!" He didn't waste time in turning the knob on the machine, which dispensed him a handful of the candy. He shoved it into his mouth and happily chewed. Almost immediately he turned the knob for another handful of candy, this one he held out to share with Sage.

"Thanks, kiddo." Sage accepted the candy. She looked like a kid herself, Cole thought, as she also shoved the small pieces into her mouth.

Kenny helped himself to another handful of Skittles, and then announced he was headed his room to watch his favorite cartoon.

"A candy machine." Evie frowned at both Sage and Cole once her son was out of earshot. "I'm going to send you two the dental bills when all that candy rots his teeth."

Cole thought about the kid's mouth. "What teeth? He's barely got any."

He watched the woman's eyes go wide and chin drop to her chest. Thinking the offhanded comment offended her, Cole considered apologizing.

"Oh, my God," Evie said, looking from him to Sage and back at him again. Then she pointed a finger at both them and laughed. "You two are exactly alike."

"I told her the same thing about her son's lack of teeth just a few weeks ago," Sage explained.

"No doubt about it." Evie smiled. "You're absolutely perfect for each other."

Cole wrapped an arm around Sage's waist and pulled her to his side. The adoring look she gave him made his heart turn a backflip in his chest.

Sage's neighbor was right. They were perfect for each other. He'd finally convinced Sage of it in Italy, and that their companies could peacefully coexist.

Now all he had left to do was persuade her to be his wife.

A knock sounded on Sage's office door, and she looked up to see Amelia wearing her smug *I-told-you-so* expression on her face, which only meant one thing.

"Prince Charming's here," the young woman teased.

Sage narrowed her eyes. "You would think you'd be sick of needling me by now."

After all, her and Cole's relationship was old news. They had returned from Italy six weeks ago, and while their days were dedicated to running their respective businesses, nights and weekends were devoted to each other. In fact they hadn't spent a night apart since reuniting in Milan, dividing their time between her home and his town house.

Sage couldn't remember ever being happier. Neither could Amelia, who reminded her daily that she'd predicted a romance between them before they'd even met.

"Nope. Never gets old," Amelia confirmed. "What was it I told you again the day Cole first called?"

The man in question strode through the door of Sage's office door. "A tall, good-looking millionaire will be smitten by her photo, fall hopelessly in love and then proceed to sweep her off her feet," Cole answered the question.

Amelia crossed her arms. "You know the rules, Mr. Sinclair," she scolded. "You're aren't supposed to come in this office until we make sure there aren't any Stiletto secrets on Sage's desk."

Cole raised a brow at the use of her actual name. *"Sage?"*

Sage watched the smug look return to her assistant's face. "Nobody calls her general anymore," the young woman said. "Ever since you two got together, she's gone from grizzly bear to teddy bear." Amelia inclined her head in a short bow. "The entire Stiletto team is in your debt."

Sage stood and rounded her desk. In an instant, she was in Cole's arms. He captured her lips in a kiss that didn't end until she heard Amelia's dreamy sigh in the background.

"Is your boss free for lunch today?" As always, Cole directed his question at Amelia, who knew her schedule better than she did.

"No. She has three appointments this afternoon," the young woman said. "And your *nooners*…uh, I mean lunches always turn into three-hour affairs."

Sage glanced at her watch and then at her assistant. There was one subject she'd retained her grizzly-bear attitude toward.

"I'm headed to class now," Amelia said.

"Good," Sage said. "Shut the door behind you."

With the door closed, Sage gave Cole a real kiss. One filled with the soul-deep passion she felt for him.

"What if I promise to be good, and have you back at work in an hour?"

Sage felt his growing hardness pressed against her. Her entire body wanted to believe him, but she knew better. Plus, during work hours, Stiletto business took precedence over sexy business. "You're always good, but we've never been back in an hour."

Cole sighed and released her. Sage retreated behind her desk, using it as a physical barrier between herself and temptation.

"I had a surprise for you, but I guess it'll just have to wait until tonight," he said.

Sage's eyes narrowed. "I hope you didn't go out and buy me anything. If you did, you'll just have to take it back to whatever pricey store you got it from," she said. "I don't want anything from you, but you."

Cole's face creased with the familiar frown that crossed his face whenever the subject came up. It was the only thing they disagreed on. "You've told me enough times," he said.

Then he leaned over her desk and kissed her forehead. "I said I have a surprise for you, I didn't say I bought you anything."

Sage opened her mouth to tell him he had better not have, but he pressed his forefinger to her lips to silence her.

"My place. Tonight," he said.

She nodded mutely.

Cole looked down at a report on her desk, and she swiftly swept it into her top drawer.

"You know the rules," she said. "We don't discuss business."

"Then I guess you don't want to tell me who your appointments are with this afternoon," he said.

Sage wasn't even sure herself. As she continued her efforts to stop micromanaging and free her employees up to do their jobs, Amelia had a more active role in determining who and what was worth Sage's time.

She leaned forward and crossed her arms on her desktop. "I'll tell you right after you tell me all about the Espresso business you handled this morning."

"Touché, Ms. Matthews," Cole said. "I'll see you tonight."

"Want me to bring Chinese or pizza?"

"Pizza," he said. "And those sexy heels you're wearing."

Sage watched his retreating back and began counting the minutes until she'd see him again tonight.

Two appointments later, she glanced at her watch, eager to get her third and last one of the day behind her. Right on cue, Amelia walked through her door followed by a man Sage recognized.

"Your next appointment is here," her assistant said. "Sean Cox of Force Cosmetics."

Chapter 18

Cole heard Sage's key in the lock of his front door that evening and looked up from the furniture he'd spent the past half hour rearranging.

"Upstairs," he called out to her from the master bedroom.

"Want me to bring the pizza up?"

"Just yourself."

Her footsteps sounded on the staircase leading to the second floor of his three-story town house, and Cole exhaled. He hoped Sage would be pleased with the surprise as well as other things he had in store for her tonight.

He met her at the threshold of the bedroom.

"Sorry I'm late." She chewed at her bottom lip.

"Everything, okay?" Cole asked, his protective instincts on full alert.

She shrugged off the question, but worry lingered in her eyes. "Just work stuff."

They'd agree on the flight home from Milan that if they were going to pursue a relationship, conversations about their respective businesses were off-limits. They were lovers, but they were still competitors.

"Well, let's see if I can't take your mind off Stiletto," Cole said. "Close your eyes."

She did as he asked. He grasped her hand and led her into the bedroom.

"Okay, you can open them now," he said, and then held his breath waiting on her reaction.

Sage gasped and a delighted expression replaced the worry he'd seen on her face. "Oh, my God. It's exactly like the one…"

"No," he interrupted. "It's the same one."

Cole looked from the grin on her pretty face to the armchair he'd had shipped here from his Milan condo.

"I'm assuming the bottle of champagne and two glasses on the table next to it are for us to celebrate being reunited with our favorite piece of furniture," she said.

The mischievous spark Cole had grown to love as much as he loved her gleamed in her brown eyes. He sat down in the chair and patted his lap. "Come sit with me," he said. "I have something to talk to you about."

Sage shed her coat and tossed it on the bed. She raised a brow. "Will I need my underwear for this *talk*?"

"For now," he said.

Sage sat in the space next to him on the large chair. "What's wrong?"

"Our living situation," Cole said. "I don't want to do this anymore."

"I don't understand," she said.

"Two nights at your place, another night at mine." He cupped her cheek with his palm, and their gazes locked. "I want us to have one place. Our place. With our kitchen, our television with our remote control to fight over and most of all, our bed to share every night."

Sage blinked. A hesitant smile touched her lips. "You want us to move in together?"

"I do. We've proved over these past weeks that we can keep our business lives from interfering with what we have together," Cole said. "But I want to share more than just housekeeping, Sage. I'm asking for forever. I'm asking you to be my bride."

The moments it took for her to absorb his proposal seemed endless as Cole waited on a response. Tears brimmed in her eyes, before a single one splashed onto the hand holding her cheek.

She kissed his hand and nodded. "Yes." Her voice cracked with emotion.

Cole reached into his shirt pocket and retrieved the ring resting against his heart. He saw Sage's eyes light up, and he knew he'd selected the right one.

Taking her hand, he slid the pear-shaped ruby, which was flanked by two diamonds, onto her finger. "I chose a ruby ring because you made red my favorite color."

"It's beautiful." She held her hand up. "I love it, and I love you." She continued to stare at the ring as the stones glittered under the bedroom lights.

"Now that I'm officially your fiancé, there's something we need to get straight from the start," Cole said.

Sage looked past her ring at his face. "You put this ring on my finger, not through my nose." She arched a brow. "You're not the boss of me."

He leaned over and kissed her sassy, red-slicked mouth. "We're partners in this life, Sage. There are no bosses," he said. "However, I am going to find you the biggest, the glitziest, the most luxurious house in Nashville."

She opened her mouth to protest, but he continued. "I'm

buying it outright and handing you the deed. It'll be yours free and clear." Cole grasped her hand and gently squeezed it. "So you will always have a home of your own that you'll never be displaced from."

She opened her mouth again.

Cole cut her off before she could protest. "This is the one thing I won't compromise on," he said. "Nor will I take no for an answer."

"I wasn't going to say no." She squeezed his hand back. "All I wanted to say was thank you, and that I love you."

Cole patted his lap. "Why don't you climb aboard and tell me just how much."

Sage's dress gathered around her parted thighs as she sat astride him. She wrapped her arms around his neck. "Will I need my underwear for this part of our discussion?"

Cole grinned. "Absolutely, not."

Chapter 19

Sage stared at the clock, watching the glowing digital numbers change in the darkness.

She was in the bed beside the man she loved and could feel the weight of his ring on her finger. They'd been engaged three days now, yet the joy she'd found in her personal life didn't keep her work worries at bay.

Force Cosmetics can be your best friend or your worst enemy. Sean Cox's words crept into her dreams and stole any chance of sleeping.

She'd been a fighter her entire life, and she'd fight this, too. She just had to figure out how. Sage lifted Cole's arm and gently extricated herself from his embrace. It was three in the morning, and she didn't want to wake him. After all, this wasn't his problem.

"I'm awake." Cole's deep voice pierced the silent night.

"Go back to sleep," Sage said. "I'm just headed downstairs to make some chamomile tea." They were staying at his town house tonight. Over the weeks, she'd become as comfortable here as she felt at her house.

Before she could get out of bed, Cole threw back the covers and switched on the bedside lamp. "I'll make you a cup of tea," he said. "And when I come back with it, I want to know exactly what's kept you awake the past three nights."

Sage sighed wearily and rested her back against the headboard. Stiletto wasn't Cole's concern. When he returned with her tea, she'd simply tell him so.

Minutes later, Sage took a tentative sip of the hot brew. Cole sat down beside her. He wore pajama bottoms and his hard, muscled chest was bare.

"What going on, Sage?" he asked. When she didn't immediately answer, he continued. "I noticed you were distracted before I proposed, but I thought it was simply a rough day at work and let it go. Now you've barely slept in three nights. Talk to me."

She swallowed another sip of tea. "It's Stiletto business."

"When you're picking at your dinner and not sleeping nights, it becomes my business," he said.

"I'm the CEO of Stiletto. It's *my* company, and *I'll* handle the problem," she insisted.

Cole took the mug and sat it on the bedside table. "You see these shoulders?"

Sage took in the breadth of his broad, strong shoulders and nodded. He patted one with his hand. "Right here is where you lay your troubles. *All of them.*"

She started to refuse again.

"Trust me, Sage," he said.

Sage closed her eyes briefly and blew out a breath. "Sean Cox came to my office three days ago. Force wants to buy Stiletto."

Cole nodded, his lips pressed into a firm line.

"You don't seem surprised." It had been the first reaction Sage had expected from him.

He rubbed at the back of his neck. "I'm not. After we saw Sean in Milan, I suspected they'd were looking to acquire both Stiletto and Espresso."

"Has Cox contacted you yet?"

Cole shook his head. "But if he's in town, I'm sure it won't be long."

Sage hadn't wanted to talk about this with him, but now that they were, there was no reason not to tell him the rest. "They're offering a quarter of the amount of money you did for it."

Cole nodded. Again he didn't appear taken aback. "First, Sean made you a lowball offer, then he also offered you the 'opportunity' to continue to run your company as their employee for a six-figure salary," he said. "However Force, as the new owner, would have the final approval over any major decisions."

"That's exactly what he said." Sage reached for the mug on the bedside table and took another sip from it. "But how did you know?"

"Because I trained him. He's doing my old job," Cole said. "What came next was a warning about Force either being your friend or your enemy."

She wrapped her hands around the mug, absorbing its warmth. Maybe she should have confided in Cole earlier. He was certainly familiar with Force's playbook. Perhaps he could have told her days ago that Sean's warning was just an idle threat and put her mind at ease.

"So he's just trying to scare me, right?"

"It wasn't a threat, Sage," he said. "It's a promise."

"I turned down the offer. Force can't make me sell my company to them."

"But they can make you wish you had," Cole said. "For example, do you remember the organic brand Naturally Glamorous Cosmetics?"

"You mean, Nature's Glam, don't you?"

"Exactly," Cole said. "Years ago, I made the owners of Naturally Glamorous Cosmetics an offer similar to the one Sean made you, which they turned down. Force started up Nature's Glam, with branding and packaging similar to Naturally Glamorous, and they threw tons of money into it. A small company, Naturally Glamorous ended up going out of business."

"B-but they should have taken them to court." Sage was outraged on the smaller company's behalf, and at the same time, terrified about Force doing the same thing to her company. "I would have sued their asses off."

"They tried that," Cole said. "Force's legal department overwhelmed their lawyers with delays, hearings and other very expensive red tape. The company went belly-up fighting them while Force's version of them is still going strong."

"It's not fair," Sage said, already knowing life wasn't fair. However, Stiletto was the only thing in the world she could call hers. She couldn't hand it over without a fight.

She sighed. "You don't think I can survive a battle with them, do you?"

She searched Cole's face for signs of hope. Instead, he gave her facts.

"Force Cosmetics has twenty-five cosmetic and skin-care brands, including their own, and forty-two thousand employees worldwide. Last year, they had eleven billion dollars in sales," he said.

Sage hands trembled as the facts sank in, and Cole took the nearly empty mug from her hands and sat it on the night table. "Whether I sell to them or not, I'm screwed."

Then she recalled Cole was expecting a similar offer for his family's business. She also remembered why his mother had started Espresso, and why it was so important for him to restore it to its former glory.

She touched a hand to his shoulder, the one he'd told her she could rest her troubles upon. "What about Espresso?"

He covered the hand she placed on his shoulder with his own. "My personal resources and familiarity with Force's tactics puts Espresso in a better position to fend them off than Stiletto." He shrugged. "But I don't know for how long."

"Stiletto's mine. I won't let anyone take it from me. I won't let them win," Sage said, the words for herself as much as Cole.

He took her hand in his. "The bottom line is I don't think either of our companies going it alone can survive this."

"I'm not following you."

Cole looked down at their joined hands, before his gaze locked with hers. "I'm suggesting we merge Espresso and Stiletto."

Sage blinked, unable to believe what she was hearing. "I thought you understood that I don't want to turn my company over to anyone."

"That's not what I'm saying at all."

"Aren't you?"

"Hear me out," Cole said.

She nodded once, fighting off the trickle of ugly suspicion creeping into head.

"I'm talking about bringing in Stiletto as a division of Espresso, like our Sanctuary spas. You'd continue to run it as you do now."

"Sounds a lot like Force's offer," Sage grunted. "Stiletto wouldn't be mine anymore, and I'd be your employee."

"It's nothing like Force's offer. I'm not talking about bringing you in as an employee. I want you to be a partner in the Espresso empire with equal interest and voting power as my family and me. I'd have to get the approval of Victor and my sisters, but I'm positive they'd agree."

Sage's journey to get her company where it was today unfolded in her head.

The sacrifice.

The struggle.

Most of all, the fact that Stiletto Cosmetics was the only thing in the world that belonged to her and her alone.

"But I'd have to give up Stiletto," she whispered.

"You'd have to *share* Stiletto, just like we'd be sharing Espresso with you." Cole's face looked hopeful as he squeezed her hand. "Share the responsibilities, share the problems as well as the successes because that's what families do. The combined companies would be a family business. You'll be family, Sage."

She listened as he continued.

"Maybe it's unrealistic to think we can take on Force," he said. "But I think you're the savviest, smartest, most innovative businesswomen I've ever met, and I believe together, there isn't anything we can't accomplish."

Realization dawned as he spoke, and Sage's trickle of doubt became a flood, overwhelming even the heartfelt sincerity she heard in his voice. She didn't like what she was thinking, but she couldn't help suspecting him all the same. "You said earlier you'd been expecting something like this to happen since Milan. Is that why you asked me to marry you? So you could finally get your hands on Stiletto?"

Cole flinched as if she'd slapped him across the face, and he dropped her hand. "Is that what you really believe?"

She saw the pain in his eyes and averted hers.

"Look at me." His deep voice lacked the warmth it had held just seconds ago. "I asked you to marry me because I love you, and I thought you loved me, too."

"I do love you."

"Trust is a component of love, Sage. You can't truly have one without the other. I trust you enough to offer you my heart, my last name and a piece of the only thing I have left of my parents, their legacy."

Cole placed his hands lightly on her arms. "Before we can take this relationship any further, I need the answer to this question," he said. *"Do you trust me?"*

The intensity in his dark brown eyes told her exactly what was at stake. However, he wanted something from her she couldn't give up. *To anyone.*

"I can't," Sage whispered.

Cole dropped his hands from her arms. The raw hurt in his eyes made her turn away as he rose from the bed.

"Then we don't have anything."

Chapter 20

Cole stared at the phone on his desk. Everything in him wanted to pick it up and call Sage, if only to hear her voice.

A week had passed since she'd placed her engagement ring on the bedside table, left his town house and his life. A week of days he'd crammed with as much work as he could and nights he couldn't sleep for thinking of her. Longing for her.

He snatched up the cordless phone and got as far as punching in the first two numbers before replacing it on its base. She'd made herself clear during their last conversation. There was nothing left to say.

She doesn't trust you.

The realization cut deep, even deeper than when he'd discovered his mother hadn't trusted him. The two women who had meant the most to him, to whom he had only given his best, had both regarded him the same way.

Untrustworthy.

A brief knock sounded on his door, and Loretta walked in. The sparkle of the earrings and necklace, he'd selected for her at the Buccellati boutique in Milan, caught his eye. She'd worn them every day since she'd opened the box.

"Sean Cox is here," she said.

"Send him in," Cole said.

The older woman hesitated. "Can I get you anything?" Her gravelly voice was filled with concern.

Cole wanted to tell her to go back to being her annoying, cantankerous self. With everything else in his life turned upside down, he needed something to remain steady.

"I'm good," he said aloud.

After an awkward greeting, Sean sat in the chair across from his desk. His former protégé was nervous.

He was about to launch into his spiel, but Cole held up a hand to stop him. "I know what you're going to say, because I taught you every word."

"Then I'll get right down to the terms of our offer for Espresso," Sean said.

"Save it. Espresso Cosmetics isn't for sale at any price, under any circumstances."

Sean eyed him across the desk. "You trained me, Cole, so I don't have to tell you what comes next, but I will anyway as a reminder. If we can't buy you, we'll break you."

Cole had used the same line himself, while working at Force. However, he'd never had it turned on him.

A phrase of Sage's popped into his head. It felt like the perfect reply. Cole leaned back in his chair and crossed his arms over his chest. "Bring it," he said.

His chest tightened at the memories the phrase brought rushing to his head.

Sean blinked. "That's exactly what Sage Matthews told me when I was in her office." He shook his head. "Wow, you two really are well matched."

Cole had thought so, too. Turned out he was wrong.

"But even with your vast resources and wealth, Force is bigger and worth even more," Sean said. "You can't win."

Their conversation gave him a momentary flashback of another one. The one between him and Sage when he'd initially offered to buy Stiletto. He'd been even more condescending than Sean.

First he and now Force had come after Stiletto. No wonder Sage was so defensive and protective of the company she'd built...*and wary*.

For the first time since their breakup, Cole wondered if he'd misjudged her. He'd gone on and on about trust, but hadn't given her the benefit of the doubt.

The man Cole had mentored cleared his throat. "I guess that concludes our business." He started to stand but hesitated and sat back down. "You know, I'm just doing my job here. It's not personal—just business."

"I get that," Cole said. "Still, I need you and Force to back off Sage and Stiletto."

"I can't do that," Sean said.

Cole found himself issuing his own warning. One he didn't know exactly how he'd back up, but he would. Even if it took every nickel he had in the bank.

"Then expect a hell of a battle on your hands in Nashville."

Sage watched Shelia retreat from her office and suppressed a twinge of guilt.

Shaking if off, she returned her attention to her computer monitor. What did she have to feel guilty about anyway? Stiletto was her company, and she would run it the way she saw fit.

Over a week had passed since her breakup with Cole and misery, along with her fears over Force Cosmetics, had resurrected her tendency to micromanage and control every aspect of her business. It had intensified to the point her employees were probably calling her worse names than General behind her back.

Sage sighed. What choice did she have? Now that Stiletto was in Force Cosmetics' crosshairs, she had to make sure everything was perfect, and the only way to ensure that was to handle it on her own.

It didn't have to be this way, a voice inside her whispered. *You had the perfect partner, and you chose to go it alone.*

She glanced down at her hand. She'd only worn Cole's ring for three blissful days. Still, she missed the solid weight of it on her finger. She missed having him in her life.

Sage's office door opened and Amelia stormed through it. "You've gone too far this time, General." She planted her fists on her nonexistent hips. "I just got back from class to find Shelia in the bathroom in tears."

"You mean the Shelia who called me names behind my back and locked me in a closet?" Sage replied.

"I thought that was ancient history, and you and I both know she's a hard worker who cares about this company. We all do, despite your making it extremely difficult lately. Ever since you and Cole broke up, you've been acting like a big…"

Sage held up a warning hand. "Watch it, Amelia," she said in the firmest tone she'd ever used with the young woman. "This has nothing to do with Cole. You know better than anyone the kind of pressure I'm under now that Force Cosmetics is looking to come after this company."

Her assistant sighed heavily. Her hands dropped to her sides. She walked over to Sage's desk. "You can't do this alone. You don't have to do this alone," she said. "That's why we're all here."

"But ultimately this company is my responsibility," Sage said.

"When you began learning to trust the team you put together to do their jobs, did they ever once let you down?"

Sage didn't have to answer. They both knew they hadn't.

"Also, did you know there was an error made last week on a packaging order from China?" Amelia asked. "We nearly ended up with a million eye shadow pans instead of a hundred thousand. I don't have to tell you how much that would have cost Stiletto."

A small fortune, Sage thought.

She was on the verge of demanding to see the employee responsible when she remembered handling that particular order herself. She'd stayed at the office until midnight that night because she hadn't wanted to go home and face an empty house without Cole.

The look on her assistant's face confirmed that Amelia was well aware who had made the error.

"But how…"

"Shelia discovered it," Amelia said. "She noticed how exhausted you were from the long hours you've been putting in here and took the initiative to double-check the order. She didn't want me to mention it to you because she knew you were going through a rough time."

Sage closed her eyes briefly. When she opened them she couldn't quite meet her assistant's gaze. Shelia had not only done her own job, she'd stepped in and done hers, too. "And I just took her head off over something insignificant," she said to herself more than Amelia.

Sage thought briefly of Cole and how much she respected him for making a special trip to her office that day to admit he was wrong. That was the day she'd fallen for him.

She rounded her desk and walked past Amelia.

"Where are you going?" her assistant asked.

"To apologize to Shelia for underestimating her and to try to make amends," Sage called over her shoulder as she left her office for the ladies' room.

Shelia wasn't the only one Sage had treated badly and needed to make amends to. She just hoped it wasn't too late.

Chapter 21

"You look like hell, son."

Cole didn't doubt Victor's word when he ran into him in the lobby of the Espresso building the next morning. After tossing and turning most of the night, he'd finally fallen into a fitful sleep only to be awakened by his alarm clock an hour later.

He'd been dreaming of Sage, all decked out in red with sky-high heels and hair as wild and untamable as the woman herself.

"Why don't you come stay at the house for a while to get your mind off things," Victor suggested. By things, Cole knew he meant his broken engagement. "There's plenty of room, and it would be good to have you at home again."

Cole appreciated the offer, but he was too old to go running home to his stepdad. "I'll be okay, Vic," he said. "How about I come out there for dinner one day his week."

His stepfather's eyes lit up. "I'd like that. It's been pretty lonely rattling around in that big house all these years without your mother and you kids." The older man shrugged. "I've even been thinking about dating again, which I know sounds ridiculous at my age."

At the bank of elevators, Cole jabbed the button with the arrow pointing up. Again, only one of the three was working. With Force Cosmetics targeting Espresso, the building issue would have to remain on the back burner for now.

"So what do you think?" Victor asked.

"About what?" Cole said absently as they boarded the elevator car.

"Your old man dating again."

"I think it's way overdue. You should have gotten back into circulation years ago."

His stepfather shrugged. "But I don't even know where to start."

With his own love life in a shambles and the woman he loved no longer sharing his bed, Cole was in no position to offer advice. However, all the older man was really looking for was encouragement.

The elevator dinged and the doors opened on the eleventh floor.

"Next time you see a woman you're attracted to, ask her out," Cole said. "It's that simple."

"Thanks. I'm going to do just that."

Cole nodded as he pushed open the door to the executive level's outer office. Victor's problem was easy to solve. Now he had to figure out a solution to his own relationship, not that he even had one anymore.

"Morning." Loretta was already at her post. She inclined her head toward the waiting area. "Someone here to see you."

A tall, honey-skinned blonde, reminiscent of Beyoncé,

sat in a chair flipping through a magazine. Familiar eyes lit up as she spotted them, but Cole couldn't place them.

Victor cleared his throat. "Well, well, well. I think it's time your old dad got himself back into circulation."

"Hold up a sec, Vic," Cole said. He couldn't put his finger on it, but something about this woman didn't sit right.

"Step aside, son," his stepfather said. "She may be a little young for me, but I've waited long enough."

Ignoring him, Victor went into waiting area. The Beyoncé doppelganger stood, towering over his stepfather. Cole continued to stare as the two talked, trying to work out in his head where he'd seen the woman before. She wore a leather pencil skirt and pumps. *Very large pumps on very big feet.*

Loretta snorted. Cole turned to find an uncharacteristic grin on her face, and then looked back at the woman his stepfather was practically fawning over.

Good Lord, that was no woman, Cole realized. It was Freddy Finch!

"You'd better stop Victor before he tries to 'put a ring on it.'" Loretta's gravelly laugh filled the office.

"Freddy," Cole called out, eating up the space between his secretary's desk and the waiting area in two long strides.

"Mr. Sinclair," Freddy slipped from the falsetto he'd been using with Victor into his masculine voice. "They're shooting my first YouTube video for Espresso today, and I thought I'd stop by and show off your sister's handiwork."

Freddy spun around, and Cole watched his stepfather's jaw slacken.

"You look great, man," Cole said. "Tia outdid herself."

"Freddy isn't short for Fredricka, is it?" Victor asked.

"I'm afraid not." Cole shook his head, his own bruised heart going out to the older man.

"Well, I'm off." Freddy leaned over and kissed Victor on top of his graying head. "Thanks for the offer. If I were a woman I'd definitely take you up on it."

Still wearing a stricken expression, Victor headed for his office, only pausing at Loretta's desk. "Not. One. Word." He growled at the secretary and went into his office, closing the door behind him.

Frowning at a grinning Loretta, Cole went into his own office. He clicked the mouse to rouse his computer and slid behind his desk. At least the Espresso Granny problem would soon be resolved.

Cole felt confident that, once Granny's makeover videos hit YouTube, Freddy and Espresso would be an internet sensation.

Loretta's gravelly cackle sounded from the outer office. Cole exhaled. She'd enjoyed a good laugh at Victor's expense, but enough was enough. He marched out of his office to tell her to knock it off, but stopped short in the doorway.

Sage.

Clad in a red minidress with indecently high heels, she stood at his secretary's desk, holding an open green-and-white box bearing the logo of his favorite doughnut shop. Cole struggled to maintain his cool while his pulse skyrocketed.

Loretta plucked a glazed donut out of the box. "He's in there," she said, so focused on the doughnut, she didn't see him standing in the doorway. "Go on in."

Sage turned toward the door. She blinked at the sight of him and began gnawing at her bottom lip. Cole watched her incline her head toward the box. "I brought you breakfast," she said, tentatively. "But I had to bribe your secretary with one of the doughnuts to see you."

"Come in," Cole said.

Sage picked up a bouquet of yellow flowers from Loretta's desk. They looked exactly like the ones he'd brought her. "These are for you," she said, as she walked through the door of his office.

Cole took the flowers and closed the door behind her. "Thanks," he said, looking at the bouquet in his hand. "It's good to see you."

"Have a doughnut?" she asked.

Cole shook his head and an awkward silence that had never existed between them before ensued. They just stood and stared at each other.

"Sage."

"Cole."

They both spoke at the same time.

"You go first," Cole conceded.

Sage looked down at the box in her hand. "I'm here to ask for a do over. I want to turn back time to the last night we were together so I can say the words I should have said, if I hadn't allowed fear and insecurity to steal my voice. My heart has been paying the price for it ever since."

Cole took the box from her hand and placed it and the flowers on his desk. He faced her. "I want that do over, too," he said. "So I can rephrase the question."

He rested his hands lightly on her arms and their gazes connected. "Do you trust *us*, Sage? Do you trust how much I love you?"

"With everything in me," she replied. "And with everything I have."

Pulling her into his arms, Cole kissed her. A soul-deep kiss that was both a healing balm for the heartache they'd caused each other, and a promise to face whatever came at them in the future *together*. When they finally came up for air, Cole reached into his shirt pocket and retrieved her engagement ring.

"How did you know I'd come here today?" Sage asked.

"I didn't. I've carried it with me every day since we broke up, praying I'd be able to put it back where it belonged." He slid the ring onto her finger and then kissed her hand.

"The only time I want that ring to move on your finger is when it's time for me to add your wedding band," he said. "Is that clear, General?"

Sage stared at the ring a few moments, then back at him. "Whatever you say, Admiral," she said.

Epilogue

"I still don't believe it." Cole said.

Sage leaned back on her new husband's naked chest after spending their first few hours as man and wife in the bedroom of his town house, enjoying their absolute favorite chair.

"That we're married?" Sage held her hand up to look at her engagement ring, to which Cole had added a diamond-and-ruby-encrusted wedding band this afternoon.

"No, that I would have given you the biggest, most extravagant wedding this town has ever seen, and you chose the judge's chambers at the courthouse."

Sage shook her head. "I told you, all I want is you," she said. "Besides, after we get the Espresso-Stiletto merger underway, we'll be spending an entire month in Italy for our honeymoon."

Cole nuzzled her neck. "I can hardly wait."

Sage tilted her head back and looked up at him. "Do you regret not making our wedding day a big splashy affair?"

"Maybe just a little."

"Really?" Sage asked.

Cole shrugged. "Then I'd have a video of the expression on the judge's face after you promised to love, cherish and *bring it* for as long as we both shall live."

"A vow I intend to keep," Sage promised again. "I just hope you can handle it."

* * * * *

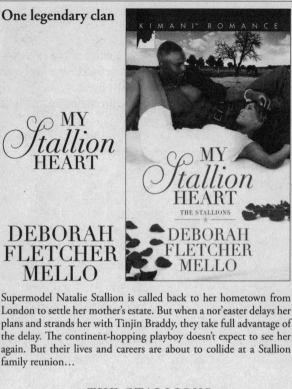

Harmony Evans

Winning Her Love

Bay Point mayor Gregory Langston wants community activist Vanessa Hamilton to help run his reelection campaign. Their attraction is a potential powder keg, especially when they are on opposite sides of a controversial issue. But a vicious smear campaign could destroy Gregory's shot at a second term. Will it also cost him forever with Vanessa?

Bay Point Confessions

HARLEQUIN®
www.Harlequin.com

Available May 2015!

KPHE4020515

REQUEST YOUR FREE BOOKS!

2 FREE NOVELS
PLUS 2 FREE GIFTS!

KIMANI™
ROMANCE

Love's ultimate destination!